AN OUTLAW'S VENGEANCE

Cody was lining up a shot of his own when he heard a terrible noise behind him. Instinctively, he whipped his head around to see what had happened.

The buggy lay on its side about a quarter of a mile distant, and Cody knew that it had been pitched over by a rough patch of ground or a hole that Hope hadn't seen until it was too late. Three figures were lying on the ground by the buggy, but they were too far away for him to tell how badly they might be hurt.

Cody saw all this within a matter of seconds, but he was distracted long enough for the remaining owlhoot to get off a shot at him. The bullet grazed Cody's skull with the force of a mule kick, blazing a line of fire and blood just above his right ear.

He hit the ground heavily. His head felt as if bees were buzzing around in it, and his vision was blurry.

He could see well enough, however, to know that Gus's remaining cohort was closing in on him, rifle ready to make the kill.

Cody felt for his Colt with fingers that seemed nerveless. The outlaw fired, and a bullet smacked the ground by Cody's ear. . . .

Cody's Law
Ask your bookseller for the books you
have missed

CODY'S LAW
Book 9

THE
PRISONERS

Matthew S. Hart

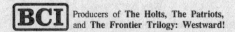

BCI Producers of **The Holts, The Patriots,**
and **The Frontier Trilogy: Westward!**

Book Creations Inc., Canaan, NY • Lyle Kenyon Engel, Founder

BANTAM BOOKS
NEW YORK • TORONTO • LONDON • SYDNEY • AUCKLAND

THE PRISONERS

*A Bantam Domain Book / published by arrangement with
Book Creations Inc.*

Bantam edition / August 1993

*Produced by Book Creations Inc.
Lyle Kenyon Engel, Founder*

DOMAIN *and the portrayal of a boxed "d" are trademarks of Bantam Books,
a division of Bantam Doubleday Dell Publishing Group, Inc.*

ISBN 0-553-29766-X

Published simultaneously in the United States and Canada

*Bantam Books are published by Bantam Books, a division of Bantam Doubleday Dell
Publishing Group, Inc. Its trademark, consisting of the words "Bantam Books"
and the portrayal of a rooster, is Registered in U.S. Patent and Trademark
Office and in other countries. Marca Registrada. Bantam Books, 1540 Broadway,
New York, New York 10036.*

PRINTED IN THE UNITED STATES OF AMERICA

RAD 0 9 8 7 6 5 4 3 2 1

CHAPTER
1

Samuel Clayton Woodbine Cody—just plain Cody to those who knew him—had for two weeks been living the kind of life that most men would envy. During the day, he had little to do other than check in at the Del Rio headquarters of Company C of the Texas Rangers to see if there'd been an outbreak of hostile Indian activities or if a new band of owlhoots was threatening the peace and well-being of the citizens of Texas. During the evening, he spent his time at the Rio Grande Hotel, playing poker and enjoying the company of Marie Jermaine, the beautiful red-haired saloon hostess who was loved by many men but who saved her affection for Cody alone.

Indeed, it might be considered by most men to be an ideal existence. Why was it, then, Cody wondered, that he was bored almost to distraction?

Most likely it was because the dark-haired, mustachioed Ranger was essentially a man of action. It was fine to sit around for a day or so, but after a while a life of inactivity began to pall. Of course there was the occasional bust-up in the Rio Grande Hotel to take care of. Some cowboy would come in and get "likkered up" and accuse someone of cheating at cards or try to persuade one of the girls to do a few tricks that weren't covered by the fee he'd paid her, and Cody would step in and see that things didn't get out of hand. The Rio Grande's owner, Ernest Palmatier, provided Cody with a free room in the hotel in exchange for his services in just such little emergencies.

But taking care of drunks and rowdy cowhands wasn't what Cody had joined the Texas Rangers for, and he was beginning to think that the Texas frontier was getting tame. That was how he put it to Alan Northrup and Seth Williams, the two young Rangers who were stationed at the desks in the front room of headquarters.

At twenty-two—though his smooth, ruddy cheeks made him look even younger—Alan Northrup was about ten years Cody's junior. He had a tendency to gain weight easily, thanks to his fondness for the pies, cakes, and homemade candy that he consumed with gusto every chance he got, but he was a quick learner, and he could handle himself in a dangerous situation.

Seth Williams was even younger than Alan, a particular fact that he didn't like anyone to comment on. He had grown up hard and fast on the Texas frontier, and he could handle a pistol, knife, or rifle as well as nearly anyone the Rangers had.

"You're just saying that because you haven't had to shoot anybody lately," Alan joshed in response to Cody's complaint.

"Naw, that ain't it," Seth called from the opposite desk. "He's just gettin' old. You know how it is when a fella gets to be a certain age. He spends all his time talkin' about how rough it used to be in the good old days."

Cody smiled at the good-natured ribbing. He knew that the youngsters were as fond of action as he was—probably even more so because they still thought of law enforcement as something like a game. They didn't yet fully appreciate the dangers that went along with it. Cody did. He had been carrying a badge for a long time, and he'd seen too many good men die. Cody understood the dangers, all right, but he also knew that a man could go stale sitting around a hotel barroom and handling playing cards all day.

But instead of pointing any of that out, he joined in the spirit of the banter. "That's right. You young whippersnappers don't know what it was like in the old times, chasing desperadoes through the snow in your bare feet 'cause you couldn't afford a horse or boots."

"Snow!" Seth exclaimed with a laugh. "Will you listen to that? You don't expect us to believe you've ever seen enough snow to walk in, now, do you?"

"Not down in this part of the valley," Alan scoffed, referring to the fact that the Rio Grande Valley was practically a tropical paradise in the winter compared to some other parts of the state to the north and west.

Seth ran a hand through his long, sandy hair, and his grin changed to a frown. "I heard somebody talkin' about that yesterday, though. Said that the woolly worms were twice as hairy this year as he'd ever seen 'em, and that's a sure sign of a rough winter comin' up."

Alan looked thoughtful. "You know, he might be right. I never saw so many birds as went over Del Rio this past fall. They must really be trying to get as far south as they can, and we've already had a frost or two."

Seth jumped out of his chair. "What do you think, Cody? Could we really see some snow down here this year?"

Cody laughed. "You two act like it'd be something special. It wouldn't, let me tell you. It's cold, and it's wet, and it makes for hard traveling for man and beast."

"I don't care," Alan said. "It'd be fun to see, just the same."

"I guess your idea of fun is different from mine," Cody told him. "I'd just as soon see sunshine and have it stay warm year 'round."

"Well, not me," Seth said. "I'd like to see—"

What the young Ranger would have liked to see never got expressed, because at that moment the door to the headquarters opened and a man came into the room. He looked vaguely familiar to Cody, and after a couple of seconds the Ranger figured out who he was: a rancher who had a hardscrabble spread a good piece northwest of Del Rio. He kept mostly to himself, but Cody remembered having seen him in town a couple of times when he'd come in for supplies. He was somewhere in his middle thirties, with a darkly tanned face. His wool-lined jacket was worn, and his jeans had been none too neatly mended in places. His dark hair was unruly and tangled where it stuck out from under his hat.

The rancher looked around the room as if he was embarrassed to be there. He took off his hat and twisted the brim in his hands. "Which one of you's in charge here?"

Cody looked hard at Alan and Seth to make certain neither of them broke out laughing. Then he said, "None of us, that's for sure. Maybe you'd like to see the cap'n."

"If he's the one in charge, I reckon I would," the man said. His eyes still roamed around the room, refusing to be still and look directly at anyone.

"Follow me, then, and I'll take you to his office," Cody said, nodding toward the hallway that led to the office of Captain Wallace Vickery.

As he walked in front of the nervous rancher he could almost feel the curiosity of Alan and Seth, but he knew that they'd stay at their posts. He, on the other hand, fully intended to hear whatever it was the man had to say. It smelled like it could be trouble to Cody, and he found himself almost hoping it was.

Cody knocked on the door to Captain Vickery's office, then opened it and stepped inside. The commander was standing with his back to the room, looking out the window that overlooked the street. He turned slowly and faced Cody.

"Mornin', Cody," he said. "There a problem?"

Captain Vickery was a powerful-looking man in his late fifties, with startlingly white hair framing his lined and leathery face and a mustache that was equally white. He wore a dark suit, white shirt, and string tie, looking every inch the frontier preacher he had been before resuming his duties as a Ranger when the force had been started up again back in '74. He was equally suited to calling down hellfire and brimstone on an erring congregation or dealing out a little hellfire of his own to an erring lawbreaker. A Bible lay on his desk, and more than once Cody had entered the office to find Vickery reading it.

"I don't know if there's a problem or not," Cody said. "But there's a man here says he wants to see you."

"All right." Vickery looked past Cody into the hall. "Where is he?"

Cody turned to see empty hallway behind him. He stepped back out and discovered the rancher standing to the left of the door, looking up and down the hall.

"You can come on in now," Cody said. "The cap'n won't hurt you."

"Didn't think he would," the man said, walking into the room. He still held his hat, and his eyes still darted from here to there.

Vickery stepped away from the window and sat at his desk, gesturing at his visitor to be seated. "I understand that you wanted to see me," he said to the rancher. "Figger you must've had a reason."

"I reckon so," the man said, looking from the Bible to the Ranger badge pinned on Vickery's suit coat to the window.

"Well, thunderation, man, tell me what it is, then," Vickery demanded.

Cody smiled. Patience might be a Christian virtue, but it wasn't the captain's long suit.

"It's kinda hard to explain," the visitor said, twisting his hat and not looking at Vickery.

"You'll just have to try," Vickery said. "You might start with your name."

"Oh, sure, I guess you'd need to know that. It's Eli Peyton."

Cody felt a sense of recognition. The name seemed familiar to him, though he couldn't quite say why.

"Reckon that'll do for a beginnin'," Vickery said. "Is that all there is to it?"

"Not exactly." Peyton looked around the office, then fixed his eyes on the floor.

Vickery turned his own stern eyes to Cody. "I hope this ain't somebody's idea of a joke."

"No, sir," Cody said. "Not a bit of it. He came in and said he wanted to see the man in charge. I figured that meant you."

Vickery looked back at the rancher. "Well, Mr. Peyton? Have you decided to say your piece?"

"I'm sorry to trouble you thisaway," Peyton said, looking glumly at his hat. "It's just that some things are hard to come right out and talk about."

"Try harder," Vickery said, his eyes snapping. "Remember, 'The wicked flee where no man pursueth, but the righteous are as bold as the lion.' "

"I reckon I know what you mean," Peyton said. "Not that I think of myself as bein' especially righteous. And sometimes the wicked've got a pretty good reason for fleein'."

Vickery didn't say anything to that. Neither did Cody. Peyton shuffled his feet and twisted his hat for a few more seconds, and then he said, "You see, it's this way. My brother's Gus Peyton."

"Jes— I mean, Jehoshaphat!" Vickery exclaimed. He looked at Cody. "Who's on duty out there?"

"Northrup and Williams," Cody said, who knew now why he'd thought he recognized the name. Gus Peyton was a notorious outlaw, wanted in Texas and several adjoining territories for a string of brutal robberies and killings. It was hard to think of the subdued Eli as having a man like Gus for a brother. They couldn't have been very much alike.

"Northrup!" Vickery thundered. "Bring me the file on Gus Peyton."

"Yes, sir," Alan's muffled voice responded.

A couple of minutes later Alan Northrup came into the room with a thick stack of papers. "Here's everything we have on Gus Peyton," he said, laying the stack on Vickery's desk. He looked as if he wanted to stay, but the captain dismissed him.

When Alan had left the room, Vickery began to flip through the papers, stopping every now and then to point out a particularly ruthless depredation. Then he looked up at Eli Peyton skeptically. "And you say this miscreant's your brother?"

Peyton nodded. "Yes, sir, he is. And worse than that, right now he's up at my ranch."

"Great God almighty!"

"Yes, sir. He came there 'cause he's hurt and didn't have no place else to go, or leastways that's what he said. Had a bullet in him that he caught when he was doin' some bank robbery. I'm a law-abidin' man, and I don't hold with that kind of thing, but he's my brother, after all, so I had to do what I could to help him." Peyton stared out the window, though it was clear to Cody that the man wasn't really looking at anything. " 'Sides, he said he'd shoot me if I didn't get that bullet outta him."

"And did you?" Vickery asked.

"I did. I dug it out and patched him up as best I could, but he's still in mighty bad shape. He needs a doctor, but he said I couldn't fetch one. Said he'd plug me if I left the house." Peyton shook his head. "He'd do it, too, do it in a second. He don't have much feelin' for family."

"But you're here," Cody put in. "And you don't look like anybody plugged you."

Peyton turned slowly to face Cody. It was almost as if he'd forgotten the big Ranger was in the room. "No, he didn't shoot me. He wasn't able. He passed out this mornin'—from losin' so much blood, I reckon—and I rode for town right off."

The rancher looked back pleadingly at Vickery, and Cody realized for the first time that Peyton wasn't precisely nervous, as he had first appeared. He was torn between loyalty to his brother and his duty to the law. And he was also scared half to death of what his brother might do to him.

"You got to help me," Peyton said. "Don't you see how it is? I don't want Gus at my house, brother or no brother, but I don't want him dyin', either. And I sure as hell don't want him gunnin' for me when—or if— he does get better. So I thought it'd be best all 'round if I came into town and turned him in to the Rangers."

Captain Vickery got up and stepped over to Peyton and put a hand on the man's shoulder. "I can see your dilemma, son. And I can tell you that you did the right thing. 'The fear of the wicked, it shall come upon him; but the desire of the righteous shall be granted.'"

"Does that mean you're goin' to help me out?"

Vickery dropped his hand. "Of course it does. And I have just the man to do it." He pointed to Cody. "This here's Sam Cody, as good a man as you'll find in the Rangers. He'll go back to your place with you, make the arrest, and bring your brother in to Del Rio."

"That's mighty good of you," Peyton told Cody, who of course had nothing to do with the decision, though he was glad that he'd gotten the assignment. Even bringing in a badly wounded outlaw would beat sitting around the barroom for another day.

"What about the bullet wound?" Cody said. "Will your brother be able to travel?"

"I wouldn't know about that," Peyton said, "but he's hurt pretty bad, no doubt about it. Soaked the bed with blood, and I had to do a mite of diggin' to get to that bullet. He can't be feelin' any too pert."

Captain Vickery looked thoughtful. "Might be a good idea to provide some medical assistance to the man. He may be an outlaw, but he's still a human bein', even if he's a mighty sorry one. What do you think about askin' Dr. Baxter to go along, Cody?"

Cody shrugged. "Wouldn't hurt to ask, I guess. But the doc's not in very good health himself these days."

That was an understatement, Cody knew. Dr. Reuben Baxter had been Del Rio's main medico for twenty years or thereabouts, and he'd done a fine job for all of that span, but the work had aged him before his time. Long rides out in cold and damp air, numerous nights with very little sleep or no sleep at all, and long hours spent standing vigil over patients who might or might not see the next dawn had all drained him of vitality. Worse than that, Dr. Baxter had developed near-crippling arthritis. He could hardly get around without the aid of a cane, and it didn't seem likely to Cody that he'd be able to make the trip to Peyton's ranch, which Cody recalled was a good distance from town.

"You're right about Dr. Baxter's health," Vickery acknowledged, "but he's the only chance we have. Otherwise, you'll just have to bring Gus Peyton in yourself"—he glanced at the outlaw's brother—"dead or alive."

Eli didn't flinch. "Whatever it has to be. He chose his own way. I did what I could for him, and I'd do it again, but I don't think he oughta be roamin' free, considerin' the kind of life he's leadin'."

"All right, then," Cody said. "I'll go talk to the doctor and see if he's able to travel. Either way, I'll get started for the ranch as soon as I can."

Peyton looked relieved and a little less nervous. He settled his beat-up hat on his head. "I'm much obliged to you."

"Think nothin' of it," Captain Vickery said. "You're the one who's doin' us the favor. It'll be a good feelin' to have Gus Peyton behind bars."

That was right, Cody thought as he left the room. And it would be fine with him to be feeling useful again.

CHAPTER
||||||||||||||||||||||||||||||| **2** |||||||||||||||||||||||||||||||

Dr. Reuben Baxter lived in a whitewashed house just on the edge of Del Rio's business district. The picket fence was leaning slightly, and the flower bed was full of weeds, two more signs of the doctor's inability to do all the things he'd once been able to do.

As Cody stood there looking at the house, the wind kicked up from the north and sent a chill right through the leather vest and faded blue work shirt he was wearing. Cody looked at the gathering clouds, wondering if Alan and Seth might not get their wish for snow after all. It sure seemed colder than usual. He was going to have to break out a heavy coat for his trip to the Peyton spread.

He shrugged off the thought, went through the sagging gate, and knocked on the front door, which opened almost at once, taking him by surprise. He would've thought it'd take a while for the doctor to get there.

Then Cody got his second surprise. The person who opened the door wasn't Dr. Reuben Baxter at all. It was a beautiful young woman with long hair so blond that it was almost white. She had dark-blue eyes, a wide, sensuous mouth, and a lithe, full-breasted body that even her frilly dress wasn't able to conceal.

Cody's hand went automatically to his hat, and as he took it off he hoped that he wouldn't start twisting it like Eli Peyton. The girl was so pretty, she was likely to have that kind of effect on him.

"Good morning," Cody said. "I, uh—"

"Hope, who's that at the door?" Reuben Baxter's voice called from an inner room. "Is it a patient?"

"I don't know," the young woman named Hope called back. "He hasn't quite managed to say." Her eyes went to the Colt Frontier revolver in the holster on Cody's hip. "But he's wearing a gun."

Cody heard the thumping of a cane, and then Dr. Baxter came into the room. "Sam Cody," he said. "Don't just stand there with your mouth open. Come on in."

Hope stepped aside and Cody entered the house.

"I'd offer you my hand," Dr. Baxter said. "However, I'm afraid I don't shake hands so well any longer." He looked ruefully at his right hand, holding the cane. The fingers were twisted, and the knuckles were enlarged by arthritis. He shook his head and looked back at Cody. "And what can we do for the Texas Rangers today?"

Cody was still looking at Hope. "Ah, well—"

"Oh, yes, I see that you haven't been introduced to my niece. Hope Baxter, this is Sam Cody, one of the local contingent of the Texas Rangers. Sam, this is my niece, Hope Baxter. She's come to help me out, now that I don't get around quite as well as I used to."

Cody smiled appreciatively at Hope, glad to know that she was going to be around for a while. There was always room in town for another pretty woman, as far as he was concerned. Marie Jermaine was beautiful, and she and Cody loved each other in their own way, but he also knew that he had no exclusive claim on her and probably never would. Not that he wanted one. He liked things just the way they were, with both him and Marie free to pursue their pleasures where they would, secure in the knowledge that they'd always return to one another sooner or later.

"I'm mighty pleased to meet you," Cody told Hope. "I'm glad Doc's going to get some help around the house. He's needed somebody to do the cooking and cleaning for quite some time now. It'll give him more time to take care of the ills that the rest of us come up with."

Hope's face reddened as Cody spoke, and when he was finished she snapped, "I'll have you know, Mr. Cody, that I'm no housekeeper."

"Oh. Sorry," Cody said, taken aback. "When Dr. Baxter said that you'd come to help out, I just naturally thought—"

"Yes, what you thought is clear enough," Hope said. "You 'just naturally thought' that a woman is fit for nothing more than cooking and cleaning and being a . . . a housekeeper."

Dr. Baxter laughed at Hope's earnestness and Cody's evident consternation. "Don't be too hard on the lad, Hope," he said. "You're probably the first woman doctor he's ever seen."

"Doctor?" Cody said.

"Doctor," Baxter repeated. "She's just out of medical school back East, and she's got as much training as I have. Maybe more. And she knows all about the latest methods and theories."

"That's right," Hope said. "I'm Dr. Hope Baxter. There are two Dr. Baxters in this house now, Mr. Cody, and if you've come here with a medical complaint, you'll find that I'm quite competent to take care of it."

"He won't have any complaints," her uncle said. "If everybody in town was as healthy as Sam Cody, I'd've been out of a job years ago." He paused. "And since I know you aren't sick, what *are* you here for, Cody?"

Cody was glad to change the subject. "I came to ask if you could do a favor for the Rangers." He explained the situation that existed at Eli Peyton's ranch and why they needed Baxter's help. "We don't want the man to die without a fair trial," he concluded. "He deserves that much, even if he's not exactly a model citizen."

"I'm afraid that I won't be much use to you," Baxter said. "I'm not even sure I could make the trip in a buggy, much less on horseback. What's the country like between here and Peyton's ranch?"

"It's pretty rugged territory," Cody admitted. "There won't be a road for a lot of the way, and I don't think a buggy could travel it."

"Then there's no way I can go," Baxter said. "But if the man needs medical attention, Hope should be able to take care of it. She can go with you."

"Well, now, I'm not so sure that'd be a good idea," Cody said.

"And why not?" Hope said, hands on hips. "Are you afraid that I'm some fragile flower from the East and that I probably can't even ride a horse?"

"It's not that," Cody lied. "It's just that, well, you never know what you might be getting into with a situation like this. Peyton might have recovered enough to give us quite a bit of trouble by the time we get there."

"I can ride a horse," Hope said. "And I can deal with difficult patients."

"I'm not talking about medical trouble," Cody said tolerantly. "I'm talking about gun trouble."

Hope glared at him. "Well, I can handle that, too, Mr. Sam Cody. I can handle anything that you or any other man can handle, and you would be well advised not to forget that."

Baxter was smiling. "You'll find that Hope is a woman who doesn't back down from a challenge, Cody."

"I can see that," Cody agreed. "But I still don't like the idea of a woman getting mixed up in gunplay."

Spots of red still dotted Hope's cheeks, but she spoke less heatedly. "The man you've told us about is wounded and needs medical assistance. You have no idea if he'll be in any condition to cause trouble of any kind. He may be completely incapacitated."

"That's true," Cody admitted. "But he's a low-down skunk, and your being a woman wouldn't stop him from killing you if he thought it'd do him any good."

"I don't see what good it would do him to kill the doctor who's come to help him. And I think we've agreed that he does need help. My uncle can't provide it, but I can. So I'm going with you, and that's that."

Cody looked at Baxter, hoping he'd rescue him, but there was no help forthcoming.

"I'm afraid she's right, Cody," Baxter said. "I'd be in no condition to help anyone after a journey of any distance, even if I could ride. It's Hope or no one."

Cody shrugged. He knew when he was beaten. "All right. I guess that's it, then. How soon can you be ready?"

"Give me an hour," Hope said. "How long will we be gone?"

"I think we can make it to Peyton's ranch by dark," Cody said. "We'll have to spend the night there and come back tomorrow."

Hope nodded. "Fine. I'll be ready in an hour."
"I'll be back," Cody said.

Dr. Hope Baxter stood at the door and watched as Cody walked away. The man's attitude infuriated her. How dare he assume that she was there to cook and clean? While it might be true that there were very few women physicians in the West—or anywhere else, for that matter—there was no reason for a man to automatically assign a woman to the kitchen as soon as he saw her.

Nevertheless, Hope wasn't surprised. She had known all along that she was going to have to change many minds about her abilities before she was completely accepted. She had met with difficulties and prejudice even in medical school, but she had eventually convinced everyone that a woman could do all the things a man could—and do them just as well. There'd been no fainting at the sight of blood, no cringing from the dissection of cadavers that everyone had obviously expected of her. Eventually the other students, all of them males, of course, realized that her determination and skills were the equal of their own, if not greater, despite the fact that she was a woman. In the end she had convinced them. And for some reason Hope felt it especially necessary to convince Cody of her proficiency as well. He might be a bit unenlightened when it came to accepting the place of women in modern life, but he had a certain undeniable appeal. Something about the way he spoke and held himself indicated to her that he was every bit as competent in his own way as she was in hers.

There was more to it than that, though she almost refused to admit it to herself. She hadn't formed any romantic attachments in medical school—not because there hadn't been ample opportunity, but because she couldn't afford the time or the emotional outlay. She couldn't afford them now, either, not when she was just about to begin establishing herself as a physician. Nevertheless, Sam Cody was a very attractive man.

Turning her mind from the Ranger's ruggedly pleasing face and tall, sinewy body, Hope turned from the door.

She had to get her things together. She had a feeling that Cody wasn't going to give her any extra time to get ready, not even a minute.

Cody sat astride the big dun and waited for the others to catch up with him. Eli Peyton was riding a wiry pinto, and Hope Baxter was riding her uncle's big Appaloosa mare, a horse that had been chosen more for endurance than speed. Hope and Eli seemed to be having a friendly conversation, and Cody wondered why that bothered him. She could be friendly with anyone she chose; it wasn't any of his concern.

He had ridden ahead to the top of a small hill to get a better look at the sky in the distance. He didn't like what he saw. The clouds that were massing in the north were heavy and blue, so blue they were almost black. There was already a chilly, blustery wind, and the dark clouds— the classic heralds of a Texas blue norther—promised that things were only going to get worse.

There was nothing unusual about northers, even in Del Rio. There had already been a couple this year. But Cody had a feeling that the one now building up was going to be something special, something that came along only very rarely. At times like those it seemed that there was nothing more than a single strand of barbed wire between the North Pole and the Texas border, and the wind that came sweeping down across the plains carried with it the very ice of glaciers and snowfields, the likes of which a native Texan could only imagine. Such storms weren't uncommon in the Panhandle, but they were virtually unknown in the Del Rio area.

Cody had seen a storm like that only once in his lifetime, and he hoped that he wasn't about to see another one. He regretted that he'd ever gone by Dr. Baxter's house. It was bad enough to be taking a woman to a place where Gus Peyton was waiting, wounded or not, but things would be complicated considerably by a winter storm, even a mild one. Cody hated to think what a genuine blizzard would mean. For one thing, it would certainly slow them down.

He turned in the saddle and called to the others to hurry along. He wanted to get to Peyton's cabin before the weather got any worse. Hope had shown that she was a good rider, but Cody was worried about how she would fare in rain or snow.

Fortunately, the rest of the trip proved uneventful. They covered some rugged terrain, and the dark clouds continued to pile up in the northern sky, but the threatened storm didn't break.

Cody heaved a sigh of relief when they came in sight of the cabin in the late afternoon. If the weather changed suddenly, they'd at least have shelter.

But even before he finished congratulating himself, the first bullet whined over their heads, followed almost at once by the cracking sound of a rifle shot.

Hope's reactions were as good as anyone's, and all three riders instinctively turned their horses back down the trail in the direction of a large rock pile they'd just passed.

"Hell's fire!" Eli said as they reined in behind the rocks. "I should'a known. That damn Gus always did have the constitution of a mule. He must'a come to and figured out I was gone for help."

"And I guess you had a rifle there in the cabin," Cody said.

"Sure enough," Eli replied. "I never thought about takin' it with me, seein' as how Gus was passed out and all."

A bullet chipped off a chunk of rock just above their heads. All three of them instinctively ducked, though there was no way the bullet could have hit them.

"He's not passed out now," Cody said. "I'm surprised he didn't just take off. He would've been better off finding himself another place to hole up."

"There's a difference between regaining consciousness and being able to gallivant freely about the countryside," Hope said. "If Mr. Peyton's brother lost a great deal of blood, he wouldn't be up to much moving around."

Another bullet whanged off the rock. "Well, he's sure able to use a rifle," Cody said. He looked around the area, trying to decide what to do next. "Is there a back door to that place?" he asked Eli.

"Sure is," Eli said. "What you got in mind?"

"Well, I'm sure not planning to spend the night out here in the cold while Gus is keeping himself warm, forted up in that cabin," Cody said. "I was thinking I could circle around and take him from behind. He can't watch both ways at the same time."

"That might work, all right," Eli said. "Course, you can't do it on a horse."

"Nope," Cody said. He assessed the area between their shelter and the house. There were only a few rocks and some scrubby brush for cover, but it'd be enough if he was careful—and lucky. "I'll have to go on foot. You two'll have to keep him busy for me."

"I don't know about that," Eli said. "Sure, he's a bad 'un and all that, but he's still my brother. I wouldn't want to have to shoot him."

"And I'm a doctor," Hope put in. "My job is to heal people, not to kill them."

"I didn't say anything about killing anybody," Cody told them. "I just want you to make him think we're all still pinned down here." He pulled his Winchester '73 from the saddle boot and handed it to Hope. "You know how to use one of these things?"

"Of course. But I don't intend—"

"I said you didn't have to shoot anybody. Just let off a shot into the air every now and then. Eli, you do the same with your pistol. You don't even have to come close to the house. Just shoot enough to make Gus think he's got us all pinned here behind the rocks."

"What about your horse?" Eli said.

"He'll stand," Cody said. "He's used to rifle fire."

"I suspect that he is," Hope remarked, taking the Winchester. "Very well, Mr. Cody. We'll follow your directions. But try not to get wounded. One gunshot victim is enough for right now, I believe."

"Thanks," Cody said dryly. "I'll try to be sure you don't get burdened with another one." He removed his silver spurs—a legacy from his father, one of the founders of the Texas Rangers—and hung them on the saddle horn. Then he slipped from the back of the big dun and moved silently away.

It took about fifteen minutes, but Cody reached the back of the cabin without incident, Gus's attention having been distracted by the regularly spaced rifle fire from the rocks. Cody looked at the door. He'd forgotten to ask Eli whether it was thonged, barred, or what. Well, it was too late now. He'd just have to kick it in. They could repair it later. He hoped that Gus hadn't stacked anything against it.

He waited until Gus fired again, drew his pistol, and then rushed the door. He raised his right foot and brought it crashing into the side of the door opposite the hinges.

The door popped open and slammed back against the inside wall.

Gus Peyton, poised at a front window, wheeled around to face the intruder, but Cody already had him covered with the big Colt revolver.

"You can drop the rifle, Gus," Cody said.

The outlaw's mouth twisted in a snarl as he stared at Cody's badge, the silver star on a silver circle that was the symbol of the Rangers and Lone Star law, and for a second Cody thought he'd have to kill him. It would've been too bad, but Cody wouldn't have hesitated, a fact that Gus seemed to suddenly realize. He dropped the rifle.

A bunk with bloody covers was on one side of the room, and Cody motioned at it with his Colt. "Sit over there."

Gus walked over to the bunk and sat down. There was a superficial resemblance between him and his brother, but Gus had a mustache and several days' growth of whiskers—and there was something in his eyes, a hint of savagery, that would never have appeared in Eli's.

When the outlaw was seated, Cody moved in and smoothly handcuffed him. "Now, lie down," the Ranger said. "You're a sick man, Gus. You ought to be in bed."

"You can go to hell, Ranger," Gus said bitterly, but he lay down.

Cody found a length of rope hanging on the wall. "This ought to do just fine," he said, and he took it over and began tying Gus to the bed.

"You son of a bitch," Gus snarled. "You got no right to tie me down like this. Like you said, I'm a sick man."

"You may be sick, but you're a little too active to suit me," Cody said. "But don't worry. I've brought a doctor for you. That wound doesn't look too good."

Gus glanced at his shoulder. Eli had done the best he could, but the wound had begun bleeding again, and the bandage was blood-soaked and dirty. "Maybe not, but I'd'a been all right if you'd kept your damn lawman's nose out of things."

Cody checked the knots. "Yeah. Well, I'd better call in the doctor anyway." He went to the front door and yelled an all-clear to Eli and Hope.

As soon as Eli entered the cabin, Gus started to turn the air blue with curses. "Goddamn you low-down son-of-a-bitchin' bastard! I can't believe you'd turn your own brother in to the Texas Rangers!"

"You may be my brother, but you're a robber and a killer," Eli said. "A man like that sorta gives up his family rights, if you ask me. Anyway, you needed a real doctor, and I went and got one for you."

Gus's snarl changed into a lewd grin as he eyed Hope. "That don't look like no doctor to me. She looks more like a little saloon girl I had me in Denver one time. Rosie, that was her name. She had those big tits on her like that, and—"

Cody was across the room before Gus could finish his sentence, and the barrel of the Ranger's Colt was pressed into the outlaw's forehead, forcing his head down on the thin pillow of the bunk.

"You've already got one bullet hole in you," Cody said, cocking the revolver. "I'd sure like to put in another one, right about here." He pressed down harder with the pistol.

"That's enough of that," Hope said, still blushing from Gus's remark. "I'll look at the wound now, Mr. Cody."

"You do that," Cody said. "And if he gives you any trouble, just jab your thumbs into some of that torn flesh on the edges of it. That'll calm him down. And if it doesn't, well, I think I'll just keep my pistol handy. You understand what I mean, Gus?"

Gus didn't say anything until Cody jabbed the pistol against his forehead again. "Yeah, yeah, I understand you," the outlaw muttered.

"That's good," Cody told him. "You can have a look at him now, Doctor." He stepped aside. There was a round red circle on Gus's forehead where the gun barrel had pressed.

Hope stepped to the bed and removed the bandage from the wound. Gus didn't flinch as she peeled the cloth away.

"I'll have to clean the wound," Hope said. "Then I'll rebandage it. But it looks as if Eli did a good job. There's no infection."

"What about him riding a horse?" Cody asked.

"He should be able to ride tomorrow if he gets a good night's sleep."

Cody nodded. "I was hoping you'd say that. Nothing like a good ride in the cool weather to get a man's blood stirring, wouldn't you say, Gus? A nice, easy trip back to town."

Gus looked sullen. "You might be surprised, Ranger. It might not be as easy as you think."

Cody didn't respond, but he knew Gus could be right. It might not be as easy as he thought it would be. It hardly ever was.

CHAPTER
||||||||||||||||||||||||| 3 |||||||||||||||||||||||||

There wasn't much Eli Peyton could offer Hope and Cody in the way of hospitality, other than a hot meal and a roof over their heads. The cabin was small, sleeping space was extremely limited, what with Gus taking up the only bed, and only one chair offered much in the way of comfort.

But the iron cookstove provided plenty of heat once they got it fired up, and Cody was grateful for that. The temperature had dropped fast with the coming of night, and the north wind was whistling around the cabin and finding its way between the spaces in the boards. It was going to be a cold one, all right, but so far there was no sign of snow or even rain. If it held off just one more day, Cody thought, they could make it back to Del Rio all right.

The hot meal was simple but filling—flapjacks, bacon, and biscuits, followed by coffee. Cody had offered to feed Gus, but the outlaw had turned surly when Cody wouldn't remove the handcuffs, refusing to eat.

That was just fine with Cody. "More for the rest of us," he said. They had all worked up hearty appetites riding in the cold, and none of the food went to waste. They had just finished eating and Eli had begun to clear the table when Cody heard hoofbeats. Eli had fed their horses and put them in the barn earlier, so this had to be someone approaching the cabin. Cody was instantly suspicious.

"You get very many visitors here?" he asked Eli.

Eli laughed. "Hardly ever get a one. Gus is the first person to drop by in nearly a month, and I don't think he came because he missed his big brother."

Cody stepped to the window and pulled aside the sun-faded flour sack that served as a curtain. Through the thick darkness he could see the figure of someone dismounting from a horse. He drew his pistol and turned to Eli, who had drawn his own gun.

"You'd better give Dr. Baxter that rifle your brother found so useful," Cody said. "Just to be on the safe side."

While the information in Gus Peyton's file branded the outlaw as essentially a loner, Cody knew that Gus had ridden with several other desperadoes in the course of his criminal career. There was always a chance that Gus had arranged a rendezvous with some of his former associates, and since Gus had already said something about Cody being surprised, the Ranger wasn't taking any chances.

There was a weak knock on the door, and a woman's voice cried out, "Help me! Please, someone in there help me!"

Cody frowned. There was no reason to suspect that a woman would be involved in anything that Gus Peyton might have arranged, but Cody was nevertheless cautious as he opened the door, keeping his pistol at the ready.

As soon as he opened the door, a woman stumbled into the cabin. She was small, quite young, and pretty enough, with large brown eyes and long brown hair hanging down in ringlets that had been disarrayed by the wind. She was wearing only jeans and a thin denim jacket over her cotton shirt, and she was shivering from the cold.

"Why, she's half frozen," Hope said, grabbing a blanket from a shelf by the bunk. "Come over here and sit by the stove."

The young woman walked stiffly across the room, her arms wrapped around her thin body for warmth. Hope helped her sit in the chair and then wrapped the blanket around her.

"Is there any more of that coffee?" Hope asked.

"Sure enough," Eli answered. "I'll get her a cup, and then I'll fry up another rasher of that bacon."

He quickly handed the young woman a cup of steaming coffee, but she was shaking so badly that it was hard for her to hold it steady. Hope had to guide it to her lips so that she could drink.

Cody estimated that the woman was about twenty years old, but her small size and big, innocent eyes made her look even younger. The Ranger holstered his pistol. He couldn't see that there'd be any danger from someone so cold and so obviously in need of help.

After she had managed to sip most of the coffee, she told them that her name was Rachel Madison. "And I surely do appreciate your opening the door to me. I don't know what might have happened if I hadn't seen your light." She drank the last of the coffee and handed the empty cup to Hope.

"This is a mighty cold night for a young woman to be out on her own," Cody said somewhat harshly. "Mighty dangerous, too."

"Yes, I know," Rachel said, and then she burst out crying.

Hope gave Cody a hard look. "You'll have to forgive Mr. Cody," she said. "He's a Texas Ranger who's come here to arrest a prisoner, and he's used to interrogating people."

Rachel stopped crying and looked over at Gus, who had maintained his surly silence since her entrance. "Is that the prisoner?" she asked.

"Yes," Hope replied. "He's badly wounded, but I'm a doctor. He'll be all right."

"Well, that's good, I guess," Rachel said dubiously. "He looks like a mean one to me." Then she looked over at the stove. "That bacon sure smells good."

"It is good, too," Eli said, handing her a plate. "You eat all you want."

"You might tell us why you were out tonight before you forget about it," Cody said. He didn't like tears any more than Hope did, but he wasn't going to let Rachel get away with not answering him, no matter how innocent she looked.

Rachel started to sniffle, but then she got control of herself. "I guess I owe you that much, for taking me in and everything. You see, my family has a farm close to Pandale—that's over to the west of here a little ways—

but it's not much of a farm, and Daddy just couldn't afford to keep all of us on there any longer. There's seven of us kids, you see, and the farm just wasn't making enough to support all of us."

Cody nodded. There was nothing unusual about that. Lots of families had a tough time making it.

Rachel ate a piece of the bacon. "Umm, this is really good," she said. Then she ate another one. When she finished the second, she went on with her story.

"Anyway, Daddy's brother and sister-in-law—Mr. and Mrs. Lawrence Madison, their name is—live in San Antonio. He's got a good job in a hardware store there, and he wrote and said he'd be glad for me to come and live with them. So I went."

"San Antonio's a long way from here," Cody said. "Were you going home for a visit?"

Rachel bowed her head. "No, I wasn't going for a visit. I was . . . I was running away."

"From your aunt and uncle?" Cody asked.

"I know it doesn't sound right, but you don't know how they treated me," Rachel said, looking at Cody with her big eyes wide. "After I came, it was like they had a slave to do all the housework for them. My aunt never lifted a hand to do a solitary thing after I got there. I did all the cooking and the washing and the cleaning and the mending."

"That couldn't have been much harder than your work on the farm," Cody said.

Rachel looked away. "Well, I guess it wasn't. Anyway, that's not why I was running away." She started crying again.

"You don't have to tell us about it if you don't want to," Hope said, with a stern look at Cody. She draped her arm protectively on Rachel's shoulders.

"That's all right," Rachel said, drying her eyes with the back of her hand. "You've been good to me, taking me in from the storm and all, and I guess you've got a right to know. It's hard to talk about, though."

She looked so young and vulnerable that Cody was almost sorry he had asked, but now that he had, he wasn't going to let up—not with the way Hope was acting.

"Go ahead," he urged, a look of suspicion on his face.

"Well," Rachel went on, "it was my uncle. He was always saying things to me when my aunt wasn't around."

"What things?" Cody wanted to know.

"Like, 'You sure are a pretty little filly,' or 'If you'd let me, I could show a girl like you a real good time.' "

Hope was horrified. "Did he ever do anything other than talk?"

Rachel shook her head. "He never touched me or anything like that. But I could tell he was thinking about it. If you could've seen the look in his eyes—"

"I'm glad I didn't," Hope said with a shudder of both revulsion and outrage.

"Well, anyway, I decided I had to get away from there, and I didn't know of anyplace to go except home. So I got me a horse and started out the other day. I was doing fine until this weather caught me. I don't think I've ever been so cold! I thought I was going to just freeze to death tonight, and then I saw the light from the cabin. If you hadn't opened the door to me, I don't know what would've happened."

"Well, now, you don't need to worry about that no more," Eli told her. "You just rest up here and keep warm, and everything'll be all right. You can stay here till the weather turns, and then I'll see to it that you get to Pandale."

"Oh, thank you," Rachel said, looking at him with open gratitude. "I don't want to put you to any more trouble, though."

"No trouble at all," Eli declared. "No trouble at all. You just make yourself right at home."

Rachel thanked them all again, and the look that Hope shot Cody said that he should be ashamed of himself for treating the young woman with such skepticism.

Cody, in fact, was himself angered by the story Rachel had told. He wished that there was something he could do about Rachel's uncle, but he knew there was no way he could touch the man.

Unless, of course, he came after her. Cody pulled Eli aside to discuss that possibility with him.

"We'll be heading back to Del Rio in the morning,"

Cody said, "but you'll need to watch yourself. A man
like that'd do anything to keep the girl from telling her
family about him. If he's gone after her, there's a chance
he might stumble on this place just like she did."

"You don't need to worry about me," Eli assured Cody.
"If that skunk comes around here, I'll take care of him, all
right. And you can bet that I'll see to it that Rachel—Miss
Madison, I mean—gets home to her family."

Cody could see that Eli had taken a liking to the young
woman, and he smiled as he thought of how things might
work out. Eli's cabin could certainly use a woman's touch,
and a little romance would brighten the rancher's life
considerably. Maybe the threatening weather was going
to have some good effects after all.

The night was long and cold, but Cody finally fell
asleep on the bedroll he had put on the floor near the
stove. Hope slept in the only comfortable chair, though
she had insisted that Rachel take it. Rachel, however,
had preferred to sleep on the floor, or so she said. Cody
thought she was just being polite. It didn't seem fair that
Gus had the only bed, but Eli said he didn't mind. He
could sleep on the floor for one night, just as long as he
knew Gus would be leaving the next day.

Cody came awake at first light and, careful not to wake
the others, stood up and tiptoed over to the window. He
was relieved to see that no sleet or snow had fallen during
the night. The ground was covered with frost, and there
was still no sun, but that didn't pose any hazard.

It was going to be a long, chilly ride back to Del Rio, of
course, but they could reach town by late afternoon even
with Gus along. Besides, the wind would be at their backs
this time, making the trip a little more comfortable though
certainly not exactly pleasant.

Cody looked around the room. Everyone else seemed
to be sleeping peacefully. Eli was snoring lightly, and Gus
looked completely relaxed.

Maybe too relaxed, Cody thought. He stepped over to
check on the outlaw, hoping that he hadn't died during
the night.

Just as Cody reached the bunk, Gus sat up. "Mornin', Ranger," he said with a crooked grin. The ropes slipped off his chest and fell to the floor.

Cody's hand went immediately to his gun. He didn't know how Gus had managed to undo the ropes, but he'd have to be tied again. Even though the handcuffs were still on, the outlaw was dangerous.

As his fingers touched the butt of the Colt, Cody felt a cold, hard ring of metal press into the back of his neck. Then he heard the cocking of a pistol hammer.

"Don't try it, Ranger," a voice said. "You'd never clear leather."

The voice was as cold as the barrel of the gun, and at first Cody didn't recognize it. Then it came to him.

"Don't turn around," Rachel Madison said. "You just keep looking straight ahead, and that way I won't have to blow your head off."

Gus Peyton laughed savagely at Cody's shock and confusion. "Good job, Rachel. You fooled the hell out of the whole bunch." Then his expression darkened. "But you took your own sweet time about gettin' me loose. What the hell took you so damn long? Why didn't you do something sooner? You think I liked lyin' here all trussed up like a goddamn Christmas goose?"

Rachel's voice changed to a pout. "Hell, Gus, don't go getting yourself worked up. It's not good for you. I could tell by the way you looked that you were hurt real bad. It seemed to me that you needed a good rest more than you needed untying. Besides, we couldn't've gone anywhere last night. It's so damn cold out there, my horse would've froze his balls off if he had any."

Gus laughed at Rachel's crudity, mollified by her explanation. "Yeah, I guess you're right about that. But we got to get movin' now. Get the key to these damn handcuffs and let me loose. It's in his right-hand pocket."

Rachel reached a hand into Cody's pocket and fished around for the key. "I wouldn't try anything if I were you, Ranger. You might make my trigger finger slip, and that'd just about be the end of you. Oh, and try not to get too excited by what I'm doing. All I want is those keys."

"What the hell is goin' on here?" Eli asked, sitting up and stretching sleepily.

"Not a damn thing, brother," Gus said. "You just stay right where you are and maybe Rachel won't kill that goddamn Texas Ranger you brought here to arrest me."

Eli gaped at them and was silent, realizing what was happening. Hope stirred and squirmed in the chair, but she didn't wake up.

Rachel laughed and deliberately caressed Cody's inner thigh as she felt in his pocket, but Cody didn't move. The pistol was probably a small-caliber weapon, but the hammer was cocked, and Rachel's tiny thumb was the only thing holding it back. He didn't cotton to the idea of trying to breathe with a hole in his neck.

After a few seconds of teasing Cody, Rachel brought out the key and tossed it to Gus, who caught it in his cupped hands. He turned it in his fingers and awkwardly tried to apply it to the lock.

While he worked at it he spoke to Eli. "Wake up that doctor lady, and the two of you get over on the other side of the room. I don't want any trouble out of you."

Eli did as he was told. Hope had a little trouble waking fully, but it didn't take her long to figure out the situation, once Eli had pointed out the gun in Rachel's hand.

"I can't believe that you deceived us like that," Hope said angrily. "You're much too young and innocent to be involved with someone like Gus Peyton."

"Haw!" Gus said, looking up from the cuffs. "She's young, all right, but she sure ain't innocent."

Even with the gun jabbing into the back of his neck, Cody couldn't resist a jab of his own. He glanced at Hope and said, "Looks like I'm not the only one who makes mistakes about people just because of the way they look."

"What's that supposed to mean?" Gus demanded. He was having some difficulty with the cuffs. No one offered to help him.

"Never mind," Hope said. "Mr. Cody was talking to me."

"Don't feel bad about being taken in," Rachel told her.

"Lots of folks are fooled by my looks. Besides, I tell a pretty good story."

"You fooled me for sure," Eli said ruefully.

"Well, it was mostly true," Rachel said, smirking. "My daddy did send me to live with my uncle, but that was a while back. More than a year. And he didn't bother me. He'd've been scared to death of doing anything like that."

Gus laughed again. "Unless he had more'n a little encouragement."

"True enough," Rachel agreed, chuckling. "I guess seeing a young woman walking around half naked all the time would be enough to have a pretty strong effect on nearly any man—and I let him see plenty every chance I got. It didn't take him too long to get the idea that I might like to have a little fun with him, but even at that I practically had to drag him into bed."

Hope was aghast. "You went to bed with him? Your own uncle?"

"Sure did. My aunt like to have died when she walked in on us, too. Probably because she'd never seen her husband having that much fun before, the way I figure it. And she made certain he'd never have that much fun again, too. Packed up my stuff and threw me out of the house that very day, the old bitch."

Eli stood silently shaking his head as if he couldn't believe what he was hearing.

"Course you got even with 'em," Gus said.

"That I did. I snuck back that night and took every penny they had in the house, and then I burned the place down around their ears. It wasn't really my fault they didn't get out. How was I to know they were such sound sleepers?" She looked at Hope. "Like some other folks I could name."

"You're worse than Gus is," Eli said sadly.

"Well, I don't know about that, but we're two of a kind, I guess you could say. I drifted around until I ran out of money, and then I was lucky enough to run into him. We took to each other right off, and we've been together ever since."

Gus finally got the cuffs off and stood up, tossing

them on the bed. He was a bit shaky from his wound but clearly glad to be free. "Yep, Rachel here's my wife. She's your sister-in-law, Eli, and she was comin' here to meet you."

"I don't believe you," Eli said.

"Well, it's the truth, whether you believe it or not. We made arrangements before my last job to meet here afterward and then drift on down to Mexico. Get us a fresh start somewhere that the law wasn't lookin' for us." He glanced at his wound. "Course the job didn't turn out exactly the way I planned it, so the family reunion wasn't quite as happy as I figured it'd be."

"It wasn't going to be just the family, though," Rachel said.

"No, that's the truth," Gus said. "What about the others?"

"Ernie and Pete and Swain should be here sometime today. We can all go on down to Mexico together."

"Now, I wouldn't say *all* of us'll be goin'," Gus told her. "I'm pretty sick and tired of my righteous big brother's company, if you want to know the truth, and I sure as hell don't want to see any more of this damn Texas Ranger. I think I'll just tie their hands with this here rope they used on me and then you can take 'em outside and kill 'em."

"Sounds like a good idea to me," Rachel said, and Cody knew she would shoot them without a second thought. There really wasn't much he could do about it, though, not with Rachel still pressing a gun into his neck.

Gus moved to Cody's side and pulled the Colt from its holster. He tossed it on the bunk with the handcuffs.

"You never know when you'll need a good gun and some handcuffs," he said. "And, Doc, you don't have to worry about a thing. We ain't goin' to kill you. You never know when you'll need a doctor, either. 'Sides, I was worried that the fellas might get jealous of me if I kept Rachel all to myself. Now *they'll* have somebody to play with, too."

"You son of a bitch," Cody breathed.

"Ain't it the truth?" Gus replied, chuckling. "But there ain't one damn thing you can do about it."

He pulled the Ranger's arms behind his back. "Matter of fact, I think I can use those cuffs right now." He took them off the bunk and snapped them around Cody's wrists. Cody could hear the outlaw's ragged breathing.

"You don't sound too good to me," he said. "Maybe you'd better let Dr. Baxter have a look at that wound."

"I got somethin' I may let the doc have a look at a bit later on," Gus said. "Least I will if Rachel don't mind too much. But it ain't a wound." He laughed lewdly and walked across the room toward Eli.

He was almost there when his step faltered and he half turned back toward Cody and Rachel. The color drained from his face, and he collapsed in a heap on the floor.

"Don't you move!" Rachel screamed at Cody, her voice going high with panic. "Don't you move an inch!"

Cody looked at the Colt on the bunk, but he didn't move toward it. Rachel might be frightened, but the hand holding the pistol never wavered.

"Now, you turn around," Rachel told him, her voice already back to normal. "Real slow."

Cody did as he was told. When he was facing the others, Rachel leaned back and grabbed the Colt. She put the little .32 that she'd been holding into her jacket pocket and covered all of them with the longer-barreled Colt.

"Now then, Miz Doctor, you help Gus. And you'd better be sure that nothing happens to him. If he doesn't walk out of this cabin, nobody will. Except me."

Hope just sat where she was.

"I'm not fooling with you," Rachel warned. "I'll count to three, and if you don't start helping Gus, I'll put a bullet in Eli's privates." She cocked the hammer of the Colt and pointed it. "You just see if I won't. One . . . two . . ."

Sweat popped out on Eli's forehead.

Hope got out of the chair. "I'll do what I can," she said. "Just let me get my bag."

Eli heaved a sigh of relief.

CHAPTER
‖‖‖‖‖‖‖‖‖‖‖‖‖‖‖‖ 4 ‖‖‖‖‖‖‖‖‖‖‖‖‖‖‖‖

Hope knelt by the fallen Gus. He was breathing raggedly but regularly, and she believed that he had simply collapsed because, not realizing the severity of his wound, he had allowed himself to become overly active and excited. She was sure that he would recover quickly, but nevertheless she made a great show of changing the bandage and cleaning the wound. When she was finished, she closed her bag, but in the process she managed to slip a scalpel up the sleeve of her shirt.

Cody, who'd been watching her closely, saw what she had done, but Rachel was too intent on making sure that Cody and Eli were covered by the Colt and noticed nothing. If Hope got an opportunity to use that scalpel, Cody thought he might be able to regain control of the situation.

Hope got her chance when Rachel stepped over to look at Gus. "You better pray he's going to be all right," Rachel snapped. "If he's not, I'll shoot your eyes out."

Hope looked up at her. "He'll be fine. He just exerted himself too much. That wound is more serious than it appears." She stood up, leaving her bag on the floor, and turned toward Rachel.

Rachel shifted her attention to Cody. "You're pretty good-looking for a lawman," she said. "It's a real shame I have to kill you, but that's what Gus said to do, and he's the boss. You can go on outside now. You, too, Eli."

Eli had started meekly for the door when Hope plunged the scalpel into the back of Rachel's gun hand.

Blood spurted from Rachel's hand as she screamed and dropped the pistol. Jerking the scalpel out, she slashed at Hope with it, sending blood drops flying and slicing through the sleeve of Hope's shirt but missing the arm.

Hope swung a roundhouse right to Rachel's midsection. The blow connected, and Rachel staggered backward, smashing into Eli and dropping the scalpel to the floor. Reacting quickly, Eli wrapped his arms around her and tried to hold her there. Gus was aroused by Rachel's scream; seeing what was going on, he made a grab for the pistol as Rachel kicked and clawed in an effort to free herself from Eli's grasp.

Spotting Gus's move, Cody lunged forward and kicked the pistol across the room, then barreled into Gus as the outlaw tried to stand. But Gus clubbed Cody in the side of the head, sending him crashing into the table. Cody hit a table leg, which snapped in two with a noise like a pistol shot, and the table fell on top of the Ranger. With the excitement of the fight pumping through him and giving him strength, Gus grabbed the table and threw it aside. His lips were pulled back in a snarl, and he was aiming a kick at Cody's temple when Hope said loudly, "I've sworn to preserve life, but I'll shoot you if I have to, mister."

Gus's foot stopped in midkick as he turned to see if Hope could back up her remark.

She could. She had scooped up the Colt from the floor and held it pointed directly at Gus. The pistol barrel shook slightly, but that merely made her more dangerous, since a nervous shooter was as likely to pull the trigger by accident as by intention, a fact that someone of Gus's experience was well aware of.

The outlaw looked wildly around the room, but there was no help coming. Eli had managed to get on top of Rachel and pin her to the floor, and though she was still struggling, kicking, and trying to bite him, she was too small to dislodge him.

"Goddamn," Gus spat. *"Goddamn!"*

"I've been meaning to talk to you about your language," Hope remarked. "It's very improper. Now, go sit on the bunk before I pull this trigger. I'd try not to kill you, but I'm not really a very good shot, so I can't make any promises."

"Goddamn," Gus said again, but he walked over to the bunk. As soon as he reached it, he collapsed once more. The battle had been too strenuous for him.

Cody stood up and looked at Eli. "You can let Rachel go now," he said. "I think Dr. Baxter pretty much has the drop on all of us."

Rachel came up sputtering mad. Her hand was still bleeding freely, and she had gotten blood on Eli as well as on herself. She glared at Hope. "You bitch! You'll goddamn well pay for this!"

"Your language is no better than your husband's," Hope said. "You'd better go over there and stand by him."

"Let her open these cuffs first," Cody said. "Gus put the key in his pocket."

"You heard him," Hope told Rachel.

Rachel clearly didn't want to do it, but she went over to Gus, got the key from his pocket, and opened the cuffs. As Cody was taking them from her she suddenly lunged at his eyes, her fingers like claws.

Cody grabbed her arms, twisted her around, and shoved her hard across the room. She slammed into the bunk and fell atop Gus, who was in no condition to complain. Rachel pushed herself off him and sat there scowling at the Ranger.

"Sorry to be so rough on a sweet, innocent girl," Cody said dryly to Hope. "Can I have my gun back now?"

Hope handed it to him gingerly. "I suppose you have a right to say that. I misjudged her completely."

"We all did," Cody said. "And by the way, thanks for what you did. That little trick with the scalpel saved me and Eli from getting our brains shot out."

"You're welcome," Hope said. "But I have to admit that I had selfish motives."

Cody understood. "Didn't want to play with Ernie, Pete, and Swain, huh? Can't say I blame you much. And speaking of those three, we'd better get a move on. We've got to get on back to Del Rio. You, too, Eli."

"Me?" the rancher said. "Why me?"

"Because I think you'd be a lot better off if you came with us. You don't really want to be here when Gus's pards show up, do you? They won't take it too kindly when you tell them what happened to Gus."

"I wouldn't tell 'em," Eli said. "I'd just say he never showed up."

"Sure," Cody said. "I bet they'd be real happy to hear that. Probably just ride right on by without another word being passed."

"Oh," Eli said after thinking it over. "I see what you mean."

"Good," Cody said. "Now, we still have a couple of problems. I don't think Gus is going to be able to ride, and I wouldn't trust Rachel on a horse. What are we going to do with them?"

"I got a small buggy in the barn," Eli said. "I don't ever use it, and it's not in real good shape. I don't even know if it'll hold up on some of the rough country we'll be coverin'. But it might, I guess."

"It's better than nothing," Cody said. "We'll have to try it."

"I sure do hate to leave this place, what with those owlhoots comin' by," Eli said, looking around the cabin. "I know it ain't much, but it's all the home I got."

"It'll still be here when you get back," Cody said, hoping that he was telling the truth. You never could tell what three men who'd pick Gus Peyton as a partner might do. Nevertheless, he tried to encourage Eli. "They might settle in for a day or two, but when Gus doesn't show up, they'll figure that either something happened to him or he went on without them, one or the other. Sooner or later they'll ride on. Then you can come back and fix things up."

"I can see you're right," Eli said, giving in. "I'll go saddle the horses and hitch up the buggy."

Eli accomplished his tasks in short order, and the group departed the cabin hurriedly, with Eli taking one last look over his shoulder as they rode away.

Hope and Cody were on horseback, while Eli drove the buggy. Rachel and Gus were crammed in with him. Rachel's ankles and wrists were bound. Gus's ankles were tied, and he was wearing the handcuffs. The buggy was cramped, but it was the best they could do. Gus didn't

appear to be much of a threat now, and Rachel seemed
to have subsided into a continual pout. Cody set a swift
pace. He didn't like the look of the sky, which hadn't
improved a bit from the previous day. If anything, the
clouds had grown thicker and blacker, and the wind was
still whistling. Cody was virtually certain it wouldn't be
long before that single strand of barbed wire gave way
and half the North Pole came pouring down on them.

He was also disturbed by the thought that the other
outlaws might show up at any time. He had tried to
question Rachel about them while Eli was getting the
horses ready, but she would say only, "I don't have to
tell you a damn thing. And I won't. So you might as well
save your goddamn breath."

Cody was fairly certain that Rachel had come to the
cabin from the southeast, maybe even from San Antonio
as she'd said, and he suspected that the others would be
approaching from that direction as well, though there was
no way to be sure. But if they did, Cody sure didn't want
to meet them.

By midday, having spotted no one, the Ranger was
beginning to allow himself to relax a little. Gus hadn't
caused any trouble, not being capable of it; Rachel
squirmed around a lot and occasionally complained
of being squeezed between Gus and Eli, but there
wasn't much she could do about it, and she seemed
resigned to her fate; and the buggy, while it hadn't
been exactly comfortable for Eli or the others, had
held up just fine and survived the roughest part of
the trip.

"Shouldn't we stop and eat something?" Hope asked
shortly after noon.

Cody shook his head. "Can't afford the time right now.
We need to get off this trail first. We don't want to be
meeting any of Gus's friends."

"Do you think that could be them?" Hope said, pointing.

Cody looked off to the southeast in the direction she
was indicating, only slightly chagrined that she had spotted the riders first—after all, he'd have seen them if she
hadn't distracted him. He was able to make out three
riders.

"No way to tell who they are from this distance," he said. "There's three of them, though, and that doesn't make me real happy. With any luck they haven't spotted us yet. Maybe they're just passing through."

Hope looked skeptical. "What was it that Eli said about visitors?"

"That he never had any," Cody said. "So maybe they *aren't* just passing through." He turned in the saddle. "Eli, drive off into that small grove of trees there."

There wasn't really much cover, trees not being one of the major features of the landscape, but the copse was far enough off the trail and just dense enough to conceal them—if the prisoners weren't able to call out to their cronies and make their whereabouts conspicuous. And Cody was going to make sure that they didn't.

As soon as the buggy was hidden as well as it could be in the sparse stand of trees, Cody rode up beside it and whipped off his bandanna. Before anyone knew what he was doing, he reached into the buggy and wrapped the bandanna tight around Gus's mouth, gagging him.

"You do Rachel," Cody told Eli as he made the knot tight. Gus sputtered and jerked his head, his eyes bulging with hatred, but Cody had effectively prevented him from making an outcry to his friends.

Eli was reaching for his own bandanna when Rachel hit him square in the eye with her diminutive fist. Her squirming hadn't been because of the crowded conditions in the buggy; since leaving the cabin, she'd been working surreptitiously at her bonds, and she'd managed to get her hands free just as the buggy pulled off the trail.

The blow wasn't a hard one, but it took Eli completely by surprise. He fell half out of the buggy, and the horse leapt forward, pulling the buggy farther into the trees and sideswiping an astonished Cody, almost knocking him from the saddle.

Rachel reached down and quickly untied the rope around her ankles before Eli had a chance to recover. Then, even before the buggy came to a halt, she shoved Eli aside and jumped out. Her legs didn't work well, and she staggered and nearly fell, but she righted herself and began running back toward the trail, screaming at the top of her lungs.

"Pete! Over this way! Swain! Ernie! Look over here, you sons of bitches!"

Hope tried to cut her off before she got to the trail, but it wasn't easy to maneuver the horse in the trees. Rachel slipped by her and emerged into the clear, running faster than ever, now that the circulation was returning to her legs, and still screaming.

"Pete! It's a Ranger! He's got Gus! Help us!"

By that time Cody had righted himself on the big dun. He dug his spurs into its flanks and charged out of the trees, quickly catching up to Rachel. Leaning down from the saddle, he scooped her up, his arm around her waist, but it was far too late. Cody could hear gunshots behind him as he wheeled the horse back to the trees, and Rachel continued to yell as she writhed in his grasp like a demented snake.

Eli provided covering fire with his rifle as Cody dumped Rachel unceremoniously by the buggy. He jumped down beside her, and Hope put the rope into his hands almost before he hit the ground. He quickly bound Rachel's hands and ankles, picked her up like a sack of horse feed, and dumped her back into the carriage.

"We've got to find some better cover," Cody said, pulling his Winchester from the saddle boot.

The thin trunks of the trees might have provided adequate concealment if Rachel hadn't gotten free and given the warning, but they weren't going to stop many bullets. Cody tried to remember the territory they had covered on the way to Eli's cabin, but he hadn't traveled in that part of the country often enough to have a very good memory of its features.

"There's some rocks about half a mile down the road," Eli said, reading Cody's mind, as he levered and fired his rifle. "Don't know if we can make it there, though."

"It's better than staying here and getting cut to pieces," Cody said. "Hope, you get in the buggy and take off. We'll cover your back. And don't worry about us. We'll be right behind you."

Hope didn't question Cody's judgment. She climbed in the buggy, grabbed the whip, and urged the horse forward. In seconds she shot from the grove and sent the buggy careening over the plains, jouncing from side to side. Cody had to admire her nerve. He just hoped the buggy would stand up to the punishment she was putting it through.

"All right," he said to Eli. "Let's mount up and get after her."

They came out of the trees with their rifles cracking, and a slug from Cody's Winchester sent one of the desperadoes spinning from his saddle. Cody didn't bother to congratulate himself. He knew that hitting a target from a running horse was mostly a matter of luck, good luck in this case.

And then there was a piece of bad luck. One of the outlaws also got lucky and shot Eli's horse out from under the rancher. The horse emitted a high-pitched scream and pitched sideways. Eli barely had time to react, but he threw himself from the saddle quickly enough to avoid having the animal fall on him. However, he dropped his rifle, and when he tried to stand, his left leg gave way, and he fell to the ground again.

Cody looked at the buggy. It was still racing along, Hope apparently unaware of Eli's tumble.

That was fine with Cody. He didn't have time to worry about Hope at the moment. The remaining two outlaws were closing in now. They were no more than thirty yards from where Eli was picking up his rifle.

As Cody turned the dun to go back to Eli's side, the rancher shot one of the attackers from the saddle. The other rider stopped, took deliberate aim, and shot Eli, who fell not far from his horse.

Cody was lining up a shot of his own when he heard a terrible noise behind him. Instinctively, he whipped his head around to see what had happened.

The buggy lay on its side about a quarter of a mile distant, and Cody knew that it had been pitched over by a rough patch of ground or by a hole that Hope hadn't seen until it was too late. Three figures were lying on the ground by the buggy, but they were too far away for him to tell how badly they might be hurt. None of them seemed to be moving.

Cody saw all of this within a matter of seconds, but he was distracted long enough for the remaining owlhoot to get off a shot at him. The bullet grazed Cody's skull with the force of a mule kick, blazing a line of fire and blood just above his right ear. He was flung from his saddle, and his fingers went limp, causing the Winchester to fall from his grasp.

He hit the ground heavily, the breath going out of him. His head felt as if bees were buzzing around in it, and his vision was blurry.

He could see well enough, however, to know that Gus's remaining cohort was closing in on him, rifle ready to make the kill.

Cody felt for his Colt with fingers that seemed nerveless, but he found that he was able to wrap his hand around the pistol's grip and pull it from the holster. The thought struck him that the Colt had never seemed so heavy.

The outlaw fired, and the report of the rifle sounded muffled to Cody's ears, as if it were coming from a great distance or as if the weapon were wrapped in cotton. A bullet smacked into the ground by Cody's ear. Dirt stung the Ranger's face, and Cody reacted by triggering off a shot.

He got lucky again. The slug smacked into the center of the outlaw's chest, punching him straight backward. He seemed poised for a second on his horse's rump, and then he flipped over, landing on his head before sprawling out on the ground.

Cody forced himself to his feet, blinking back the blood that dripped into his right eye from the bullet crease. He stood for a second to get his balance; then, still wobbly, he shoved his Colt back into the holster and looked for Eli.

The rancher lay a few feet away, the left side of his coat and shirt stained dark by blood. Cody took a deep breath and walked over to the rancher. Eli's chest moved slowly up and down. He was alive, at least, though Cody couldn't tell how serious the wound was. It might have gone straight through, or it might have hit some vital organ. Hope would have to see what could be done about it.

Cody checked the fallen desperadoes. Neither was breathing, and for a fleeting second Cody was struck by the irony of the fact that he didn't know which of them was Pete or Swain. Or Ernie, for that matter. Another dead man was back there somewhere. There was nothing that Hope could do for them.

Hope! Cody suddenly remembered the wrecked buggy. He turned and saw that the buggy was still on its side, the passengers still unmoving.

The big dun was standing patiently, but Cody didn't think he could pull himself into the saddle. Maybe he could walk to where the buggy was, see if there was anything he could do. *Hope,* he thought again. She couldn't be dead. She just couldn't be. Cody staggered toward the toppled buggy. He tried to hurry, but his legs didn't seem to want to hold him up and his knees felt as weak as water. The bees were still buzzing in his head, and he wondered if the day was getting darker all of a sudden.

Deep within his mind he knew that wasn't it, that he was about to pass out or maybe even die. But he told himself he couldn't do that. He had to get to Hope, had to make sure that she was all right.

He went down on one knee and almost fell forward on his face, but he drew a final reserve of strength from somewhere and drove himself to his feet.

Cody managed to get another ten yards before he fell. This time he couldn't get up. Before he slipped into a pool of frigid darkness, his last thought was of Hope.

CHAPTER 5

Cody awoke, not sure whether he was dead or alive.
If he was dead, he thought, he was probably in hell, because he was very warm. But it was a pleasant warmth. He wasn't uncomfortable at all. If he were in hell, he'd probably be a lot hotter than he was right now.

But he didn't think he was in heaven, either. He was pretty sure he couldn't be, because heaven would be tranquil, and there was anything but tranquility. True, there were no longer any bees in his head, but it seemed as if there were someone inside there pounding on an anvil. The thought of the anvil brought to mind the time he'd spent playing the part of a blacksmith in Eagle Pass. He hoped that no matter where he was, heaven or hell, either one, he wouldn't ever have to wear a derby hat again.

He decided that he'd just keep his eyes closed for a little while longer, hoping that the pounding would ease up. But it didn't. He figured he might as well see where he was and quit wondering about it.

He opened his eyes and saw that he was lying on top of the covers of a large four-poster bed in an unfamiliar room, his head sunk deep in a feather pillow. Did they have bedrooms in heaven? In hell? Somehow he didn't think the accommodations in either place would be exactly like this. He looked around the room. A washstand with a big pitcher and bowl sitting on top was by the bed, an ornate dresser graced the opposite wall, and a cushioned straight-backed chair stood in one corner. The room was warmed by a small fireplace on one wall, and several logs crackled and burned on the grate, filling the room with the faint odor of woodsmoke.

There was nothing at all unusual about the place. It seemed to be just an ordinary room in an ordinary house.

But if that was so, where was the house located? And how had he gotten here?

He put a hand to his head, very carefully, and felt a cloth bandage. It was only then that he remembered the bullet wound and the gun battle with the three men, and as he thought about that, he remembered Eli and the prisoners.

And he remembered Hope.

He threw his legs off the side of the bed and attempted to stand, but he was so dizzy that he had to sit back down on the edge of the bed.

While he sat there he noticed that there was light coming into the room through a curtained window, and he wondered with sudden panic how long he'd been unconscious. He had to find out what had happened to the others. His feet were bare except for a pair of socks, and he looked around for his boots. They were beside the bed, and he reached down for them, fighting off a wave of nausea. Pulling the boots over, he forced his feet into them. Then he stood up again.

He didn't feel much better than he had the first time, but he thought he could make it to the door. He was about to take his first step when the door swung open and a beautiful, auburn-haired young woman walked into the room.

Cody had never seen her before.

She had a richly curved body, flawless skin, red lips, and eyes the color of the sky on a perfect summer day. She smiled when she saw that Cody was awake and standing by the bed.

"I didn't think you'd be conscious yet," she said. Her voice was low and musical. "I'll go tell Father that you're out of bed."

She had closed the door and left the room before Cody could recover from his surprise at her sudden appearance, much less say a word to her.

He wondered again just what was happening to him. Maybe he was in heaven, after all. The woman was certainly pretty enough to be an angel, and she'd sure said

"Father" in the tone that some people reserved for speaking of the Lord—though Cody had never exactly thought of angels as having bodies like hers. *Maybe I'd better just sit down and rest for a minute,* he thought. *Maybe if I do that, somebody'll come in here and tell me what's happening.*

He didn't have to wait long.

There was a light tap on his door, and a man entered the room. He looked nothing at all like the woman. Tall and handsome, with a powerful-looking upper body, he was wearing a black wool suit, white shirt, and string tie. He was probably about fifty years old, Cody thought, though he couldn't be sure about that. The man had piercing black eyes and black hair touched with silver in the sideburns and at the temples. The hair was combed straight back on the top and sides, emphasizing the man's sharp widow's peak. He also had a well-groomed mustache and a goatee.

If that man is who he looks like, I'm definitely not in heaven, Cody thought.

The man walked quickly to the bed and stood over Cody. "I'm Hayden Carswell," he said, putting out a hand.

The complete normality of the greeting made Cody feel better immediately, and he shook the man's hand without rising from the bed. "Sam Cody," he said. "Just call me Cody."

Carswell smiled. "I will indeed, Cody. I always like to cooperate with the Texas Rangers, and I'd like to welcome you to my house. I expect that right about now you're wondering how you came to be here."

Cody was actually wondering how Carswell knew that he was a Ranger, but then it dawned on him that he was wearing his badge. This was one of those rare assignments when he hadn't been on an undercover mission.

"I'd rather know about the people who were with me," Cody said. "Eli Peyton and Hope—Dr. Baxter."

"They're here, too," Carswell informed him. "And both are doing just fine, I might add. Dr. Baxter was stunned by her fall when the buggy she was driving crashed, and Mr. Peyton was wounded by one of the gunmen who attacked you, but neither of them was seriously injured. Peyton suffered a clean flesh wound, and luckily for him Dr. Baxter had recovered enough to attend to it even before anyone arrived on the scene. He's in the room next to this one, as a matter of fact, sound asleep and out of danger."

Cody was glad to hear that Eli was all right, and he was more than a little amazed at the relief he felt on hearing that Hope hadn't been seriously hurt. Was it the effect of his own wound, or did his feelings for her already amount to more than he would've thought possible? Well, he'd worry about that later on. Right now he had to find out about Gus and Rachel.

He asked after them.

"Ah, yes. Your prisoners," Carswell said, pulling at his goatee. "They, too, are doing well, thanks to Dr. Baxter. The man's wound was opened again by his fall, but the doctor ministered to him. She tells me that his condition is now stable. His young wife got a pretty hard knock on the head—nothing comparable to yours, of course—but she is apparently quite resilient. Not exactly polite, not exactly thankful for her rescue, but certainly resilient."

That pretty much agreed with Cody's own assessment of Rachel. She seemed to him to be the kind of woman who'd be able to survive just about anything. Her loyalty to herself appeared to be so great, in fact, that Cody was mildly surprised by her allegiance to Gus.

"As for how you got here," Carswell went on, "one of my daughters was out riding and heard gunshots. She investigated and came across the scene of what looked like a titanic battle. Bodies strewn all over the field. She fetched the rest of us, and we rode out and brought you here. There were some others there that we didn't bother with. But then, they were beyond needing our help."

"Friends of Rachel and Gus," Cody told him. "They didn't take to the idea of their pards being hauled down to Del Rio and thrown in the hoosegow."

Carswell nodded knowingly. "I can see why you feel they belong there, however. They are not exactly pleasant people."

"The sooner those two are behind bars, the better I'll feel about them," Cody said. "I really appreciate what you've done for us, Mr. Carswell, and I'm sorry that we've put you to so much trouble, but we'll be moving on as soon as I can sit a horse." He stood up. "I'm feeling better already. Not near as dizzy as I was at first. I think I'll be ready to ride as soon as Eli wakes up."

Carswell smiled and shook his head. Stepping to the window, he pulled aside the curtain and told Cody to look out.

The Ranger did as Carswell asked and beheld a sight from the second-floor window like nothing he'd ever seen before.

A glittering field of ice, covered in places with a thin dusting of snow, surrounded the house. The sun sparkled off it for as far as Cody could see. Icicles hung from the eaves of the house and barn, and the fence posts and the few trees around the property were encased in a radiant sheen of ice.

Cody blinked and put a hand over his eyes to shield them from the glare. "Good Lord. When did that happen? How long was I out, anyway?"

Carswell laughed. "To answer your first question, it happened last night. A storm the likes of which I've never seen roared through here not long after dark. The sleet sounded like pistol shots hitting the roof, and I feared for the glass in the windows." He waved a hand at the scene outside. "When we got up this morning, this awaited us."

"Which means—"

"That you've been unconscious for the better part of twenty-four hours. Not exactly surprising, according to Dr. Baxter. That bullet ran right along the side of your skull. A quarter of an inch to the left and you wouldn't be talking to me right now."

Cody shrugged. It was an appalling thought, maybe, but it was far from the first time that he'd had a close brush with death. He was a lot more concerned with getting Gus and Rachel back to Del Rio than with what might have been.

"Traveling won't be easy in this weather," he mused.

"Indeed it won't," Carswell agreed. "I doubt that you could get very far on that ice without an accident of some kind. And I have some worse news for you along those lines as well."

Cody wondered what could be worse, but he couldn't think of anything. So he asked.

"The buggy that Dr. Baxter was driving was severely damaged. One wheel was completely destroyed. We brought the wheel so that we could attempt to repair it, but we had to leave the buggy where it was."

"I see," Cody said.

"And that's not all," Carswell said. "The sun might be shining, but it's still well below freezing out there. It might be a while before all that ice melts."

Cody was eager to leave. He didn't trust Gus not to make trouble, and he trusted Rachel even less. But there was nothing he could do about the weather. He could make one suggestion, however, and he did so. "I think it might be a good idea to keep my prisoners in separate rooms, if you have the space," he said. "Separate *locked* rooms. They're a whole lot trickier and meaner than they look, and I wouldn't want any harm coming to you folks. It wouldn't be right for you to be brought to harm by the very people you've taken in and helped."

Carswell let the curtain fall back to cover the window. "That is most considerate of you, Cody. As you'll see when you're up and around, this is a very large house, and we do indeed have several extra rooms. And you can rest secure in the knowledge that your prisoners have already been provided with separate, and locked, accommodations. But you and Mr. Peyton and Dr. Baxter are to consider yourselves our guests. As such, you can make yourselves at home and have the run of the house."

"That's mighty nice of you," Cody said. "I appreciate your hospitality, and I know the others do, too."

"So they've said. And now, if you'll excuse me, I have to go and check on my family. You'll be meeting them when you join us for dinner." Carswell started for the door, but before he reached it he turned back to Cody. "There is one thing. We keep the upper story of the house closed—this house has far more space than our needs warrant—and so those rooms are left unheated. It would be better if you didn't stray up there."

"Thanks for the warning," Cody said. "I won't be heading in that direction. I don't want to be any colder than I am right now."

"Very good," Carswell said. "And now I suggest that you take off those boots and rest for a while. Miss Baxter is busy at the moment, but I'm sure she'll want to see you later. She has been most anxious about your condition."

Cody felt his face flush as if the room had suddenly gotten considerably warmer—but Carswell didn't seem to notice any change in the temperature. He left without saying anything more.

The Ranger took off his boots and lay back on the bed, thinking about Hope. Why did the mention of her concern for him cause his temperature to rise?

It was an easy question to answer. She was beautiful, for one thing, and in the short time he had known her, she'd shown that she wasn't only a good doctor, she was also brave, quick on the uptake, and full of common sense.

What more could you ask from a woman—or from a man, either, for that matter? When he'd collapsed on the plains, not knowing if he was dying or not, not knowing if Hope was already dead or not, he had thought he might never see her again, and that thought had filled him with immense regret. He recalled wishing that he'd taken the opportunity to get to know her better when he had had the chance, and he promised himself to remedy that situation as soon as he could. As his eyes began to close Cody thought fleetingly about the red-haired beauty Marie Jermaine, but she was back in Del Rio, and because of the ice storm it suddenly seemed a world away from where Cody was now.

Besides, he told himself, Marie would understand. He was still telling himself that when he fell asleep.

The next time Cody opened his eyes, Hope was sitting on the side of the bed, looking at him.

He realized that he no longer felt the pounding in his head, and his thoughts were much clearer than they had been. There was none of the earlier confusion about where he was or what had happened to him. He smiled at Hope, and she smiled in return.

"Thanks for taking care of me," he said, touching the bandage as he sat up.

"It wasn't a deep wound," Hope responded. "But the bullet caused a mild concussion. It wasn't really so bad."

Cody remembered the impact of the bullet. "It felt bad enough to me. I guess I was lucky."

"It's a good thing you have a hard head, all right. As if I couldn't have guessed that you did," she added dryly.

Cody smiled ruefully. "I think we got off to a bad start, Dr. Baxter. If you'll forget what I said about cooking and cleaning, I promise never to say anything about how you got taken in by Rachel Peyton—if that's really her name."

Hope pretended to think about it. "I might be able to forget what you said if you'll just admit what a good doctor I am."

"There's not much doubt about that," Cody said. "I'm not sure whether me or Eli or Gus would even be here if it weren't for you and your doctoring."

Hope smiled. "Well, thank you very much. And for saying it so well, I'll let you call me Hope. Dr. Baxter sounds so formal and stuffy."

"That sounds fine to me. And you can call me Cody."

Hope put her hand on Cody's. "Why not Sam? Isn't that what my uncle called you?"

"My whole name's Samuel Clayton Woodbine Cody. I figure if we're going to whittle it down at all, we might as well go the whole hog."

"All right," Hope said. "Cody it is." She looked around the room. "A comfortable place, isn't it?"

Cody heartily agreed. "It sure is. We were lucky to be found by anybody at all, but to be found by somebody living in a place like this is almost too good to be true. If you have to weather an ice storm, I can't think of a better place to do it in."

"Have you met any of the family yet?" Hope asked.

"Just Mr. Carswell. He seems like a nice enough fella. Seemed almost pleased to have us here. Maybe he's glad of the company. Apparently they have plenty of room to take care of us—and Gus and Rachel, too, the way he talked."

Hope nodded. "It's a huge house, all right, though it seems strange to have built it out here in the middle of nowhere." Her hand still rested on Cody's. "Are you sure Mr. Carswell is the only family member you've met?"

"Well, now that you mention it, there was somebody else," Cody said. "But I wouldn't exactly say I met her. Saw her, is more like it."

"And which one did you see?" Hope asked.

"I don't get it."

Hope removed her hand. "I think you do."

"Oh. Well, she was pretty, I reckon, but that's about all I can say. She didn't even stay in the room long enough to tell me her name."

"What color was her hair?" Hope asked.

Cody still didn't really get it. "Her hair?"

"Don't be obtuse. You know what I mean. Was she a redhead? A brunette?"

"I wouldn't call it red," Cody said.

"Auburn, then?"

Cody wasn't sure of the color, but he said, "I guess that was her. Why?"

Hope shrugged. "Nothing, really." She stood up. "I've got to go look in on Eli and Gus now. You aren't my only patient, you know."

"I know. But I do wish you could stay here a little longer."

"Maybe next time." Hope reached out and touched Cody's cheek. "I have to admit that I have a special interest in your welfare."

Cody felt his face getting even hotter than it had when Carswell had mentioned Hope's desire to see him.

"Are you getting a fever?" Hope asked.

"I don't think so. I think it must be something else."

Hope smiled. "Maybe we can talk about that later," she said, and then she turned and was gone.

Cody lay on the bed, thinking. Not primarily about Hope, but about what she had said to him. Evidently there was more than one female Carswell in the house, and there was something about them that bothered Hope.

Cody wondered if she could be jealous, but as much as he might wish that was the case, it didn't seem very likely to him. What else could it be, though? There didn't seem to be anything sinister about Mr. Carswell to Cody, and the woman he had seen, while prettier than the average, maybe, had seemed perfectly normal in all other respects. Anyway, what really mattered was that he needed to get his prisoners back to Del Rio as soon as he could. The ice storm was an unwelcome delay, but it shouldn't be a long one. The temperature wasn't likely to stay below freezing for very long, surely not for more than a day or two, and then they could be on their way.

Cody thought again about the woman who'd come into his room and about Hope's implication that there were others like her in the house. He smiled slyly. Dinner might prove to be quite an experience. It was an interesting thought to drift away to sleep on.

CHAPTER
||||||||||||||||||||||||||| **6** |||||||||||||||||||||||||||

Cody was summoned to dinner by a different woman from the one who had appeared in his room earlier. This one was a redhead like Marie Jermaine, taller than her sister, but no less attractive and certainly no less well curved, and her glittering green eyes seemed almost to promise a devilish nature, one that welcomed any kind of excitement. As Cody followed her from the room he could smell some delicious aromas drifting up from the dining room on the first floor of the house, and he realized for the first time how hungry he was.

Beautiful women and good food . . . There could be a lot worse places than the Carswell house to be stranded in the wintertime, he thought.

Dinner was served at a long table in a large room lit by lamps, candles, and a crackling fire, and Cody discovered that there were four Carswell sisters. The redhead who had led him to the dining room was named Francesca, while the auburn-haired woman he had seen in his room earlier that day was Diana. Also at the table was Phoebe, a dark-eyed brunette who wore her curly hair cut short. "She's the tomboy of the family," Hayden Carswell explained as he made the introductions. "It wasn't easy for us to persuade her to wear a dress to dinner. She usually prefers riding pants and a shirt."

Cody got the impression that Phoebe would be attractive no matter what she wore; in a dark blue dress, her white shoulders bare, she was certainly the equal of her older sisters.

The youngest of the sisters was called Brenna. Her hair

was dark, like Phoebe's, but it was long and hung almost to her waist. Her black eyes seemed to Cody to hint that she was wise beyond her years.

"They inherited their beauty from my late wife," Carswell said proudly. "And they are a joy and a comfort in my old age."

Carswell didn't look that old to Cody, but he didn't mention the fact. He was too shocked to speak when he realized who the fifth woman at the table was.

It was Rachel Peyton.

"I hope you don't mind," Carswell said without any real hint at apology. "It seemed cruel to keep Mrs. Peyton locked in her room when she could as easily join us here at the table. She's promised me that she'll be on her best behavior. Isn't that right, my dear?"

Rachel, who was looking down at the table, merely nodded.

"I reckon it's all right," Cody said, thinking that Rachel wouldn't be likely to try anything as long as the weather was so bad. "Where's her husband?"

The question was answered by Hope, who had just come into the room followed by Eli Peyton, who walked somewhat stiffly and awkwardly because of the wound in his side.

"Gus isn't able to get out of bed," Hope said. "He's not doing as well as I had thought. He lost a lot of blood to begin with, and then the wound was opened again—twice. I still think he'll be all right, but maybe it's just as well this storm came along. It will give him extra time to recover."

"It's an ill wind, as they say," Carswell intoned. "And now, let us have the blessing." The Carswells bowed their heads piously, and Cody followed suit, though he didn't look down at his folded hands. Instead he kept a surreptitious eye on Rachel. He wasn't going to take the chance of her slipping a knife up her sleeve while she was unobserved.

"Amen," Carswell said when he finished saying grace. "And now, shall we eat? I'll carve." He set himself to work on a large roast, and when he had sliced off a piece for each diner, he put it on a plate and sent it around the table.

The meal went pleasantly. There were canned tomatoes and peas to go with the meat, and freshly baked bread. Cody found himself wondering if the Carswells had taken out the good silver and china for their guests or if they always dined so lavishly. Though he was seated between Hope and Eli, Cody took the opportunity to talk to the Carswell sisters as well. He also kept an eye on Rachel, who didn't choose to join in the conversation, though she ate as much as anyone.

The sisters were as charming as they were pretty, and there was nothing about them that aroused Cody's suspicions. He concluded that Hope's earlier reaction to them had indeed been inspired by jealousy, which he thought boded well for future relations between the two of them.

But if Hope was still jealous, she gave no indication of it at dinner. She talked brightly and appeared practically to have become friends with all four sisters.

Eli was another story altogether. It was clear that he had never before been in the company of so many attractive females at one time. He wore a gooney sort of smile all through the meal as if unable to believe his good fortune. He blushed when they spoke to him and replied awkwardly, and Cody several times caught him giving the women admiring glances when he thought they weren't looking.

Cody was certain that Eli would be paying a visit or two to the Carswell house as soon as he returned from his trip to Del Rio. In fact, Cody wouldn't be surprised if Eli asked to stay behind to recuperate for a few days when the others left. There was really no reason for him to go to Del Rio now, not with Gus's three partners out of the picture. Cody wouldn't blame Eli a bit for staying around; it was what he would do himself if he could.

After the meal, topped off by apple pie and coffee, was finished, Cody felt uncomfortably full. The fireplace had warmed the room a bit too much for his taste as well, and he had a craving for some fresh air, no matter how cold it was outside.

"I'll step out with you," Carswell told him when he expressed his wish. "I should check on the livestock in the barn; make sure that they're all fixed for the night.

Just let me get my hat and coat. I'll fetch yours, too."

The others were content to remain in the dining room, talking and sipping their coffee, so Cody and Carswell bundled up and left them there, but not before Cody had whispered to Hope and Eli to be sure to keep an eye on Rachel.

Once outside, Cody took a deep breath. The frigid air burned into his lungs, and the moonlight on the ice gave the world a ghostly glow like nothing Cody had ever experienced. It was quite a sight, like something out of a picture book.

There was very little wind now, but the cold was intense. Cody could feel it seeping through his denim pants and his thick coat, and it was especially fierce on the place where the bullet had scraped his head. He resisted the urge to tug his Stetson down farther to ward off the biting cold and instead pulled up his coat collar.

When he and Carswell had walked a few yards from the house, going slowly and carefully so as not to slip on the ice and fall, Cody turned to get a good look at the place. It was a hulking three-storied structure with a wide porch that went around three sides. It looked as big as the Rio Grande Hotel, and suddenly Cody thought he recognized it.

"Is this the old Patton house?" he asked.

Carswell hesitated for a moment. Then he said, "It is indeed. Did you know Mr. Patton?"

"Nope. I never met the man. Heard about him, though. He came out here and started up in the ranching business a long time back. Did pretty well at first, from all I hear. He must have, to be able to build a house like that."

"It's a fine house," Carswell agreed. "But Patton's luck didn't hold."

"It sure didn't. But not because he wasn't a hard worker, or so I'm told. He got sick, and there was some trouble with a crooked foreman. . . . I don't know exactly what. Anyway, he had to go off to the hospital in San Antonio, and he never came back. I don't know if he died or not, but there wasn't much to come back to, anyway. The foreman had ruined him by that time."

"A sad tale," Carswell said. "But not an uncommon one."

"I reckon not. The last time I came through these parts, that old house was empty. Some of the windows were broken, and birds were nesting in the place. You've done a good job of fixing it up."

"It was hard work, but it was worth it," Carswell told him. "My family's never been afraid of a little work."

"What brought you here?" Cody asked. "It's kind of out of the main way of things."

"That's the way I like it," Carswell said. "It keeps us away from the temptations of the city, and that's something to take into consideration when you have four daughters as pretty as mine."

"You've lived in the city, then?"

"We've moved around a good deal, looking for the proper place to settle," Carswell said vaguely, not exactly answering the question. "I think we've found it now." A horse whinnied, and Carswell turned toward the barn. "I'd better tend to the livestock. It sounds as if they're waiting for me."

Cody watched him go. He wondered if Carswell's daughters found the place as attractive as their father seemed to. They looked like lively young women, and he couldn't understand why they'd want to live so far from the entertainment of a city or the prospect of meeting eligible young men.

But maybe he was being guilty of making the kind of judgments that Hope had accused him of earlier. Maybe not every young woman, no matter how beautiful she was, would be looking for a husband or for the social life a city could offer.

He slapped his arms against his body for warmth and decided that it was time to go back inside. The moonlight on the ice was a pretty sight, all right, but only a fool would stand out here and freeze to death while he was looking at it.

Hayden Carswell stood in the barn door and watched Cody make his way back to the house. He supposed that the Ranger had a right to ask his questions, but he wasn't a man who liked for others to pry into his personal affairs, and it didn't much matter to him whether the one doing the prying was a lawman or not.

He had seen the way Cody looked at his daughters, too, and he didn't blame him for that. They were mighty fine-looking women, if Carswell did say so himself, and they'd been brought up right, to respect their father and follow the rules he laid down for them. They understood how it was when a man didn't choose to live cooped up in a town like other folks and follow their ways, and they had accepted Carswell's decisions dutifully ever since they were youngsters.

He went on into the barn. It was a bit warmer in there than it had been outside, but not by much. The horses were stamping in their stalls, trying to keep warm, and Carswell thought he might lay blankets across their backs for the night, make them a little more comfortable. He was a man who believed in kindness to animals, just as his daughters did. Yes, indeed, he thought, he was just a simple man of goodwill who wanted to be left alone to live his life according to his own lights, even if that meant living in a way that was mighty unconventional by most standards, and he wasn't worried that the Ranger would do anything to change that.

No, sir. He wasn't worried about that at all.

When Cody returned to the house he found the dinner conversations had broken up, and the dining room was deserted. He found his way back to his bedroom without seeing anyone, and he was about to enter it when Hope put her head out of a door just down the hall.

"I thought I heard you come in," she said softly. "There's something I'd like to talk to you about."

Cody liked the idea of talking to Hope; actually, he wouldn't have minded if they did more than talk. "Just let me shed this coat and I'll be right there."

He went into his room and took off his coat and Stetson, tossing them on the chair in the corner. Someone had laid a new fire in the fireplace, and the room was filled with a comfortable warmth. But Cody didn't linger to enjoy it. He was eager to talk to Hope.

He rapped lightly on her door, and she opened it at once. He had hardly gotten inside before she asked him, "Now that you've seen all of them, what did you think of the Carswell family?"

There were two small wing chairs in Hope's room, both of them a lot more comfortable looking than the chair in Cody's room. He sat down in the one nearest the stove and propped his right foot on his left knee. The warmth from the stove felt very good after his outing.

"Those sure are four pretty women," he said when he had gotten settled. "They don't look very much alike, though. Hard to believe they're sisters."

Hope gave him an exasperated look as she settled in the other chair. "That's not what I meant, and you know it."

He remembered the odd way she had behaved that afternoon. "Maybe you'd better tell me just exactly what you mean. Make it easy for me. You have to remember, I got shot in the head yesterday."

"That's just it," Hope said with a frown. "I don't *know* exactly what I mean."

Actually, Cody understood the feeling. He'd been having it himself ever since his conversation with Carswell outside the house. He tried putting it into words.

"Everyone here's treated us like we were long-lost friends," he said. "They've put us up, fed us, and gone out of their way to see that we're comfortable. But there's still something about them that just doesn't seem right. I can't put my finger on it any more than you can, but I can feel it."

"I wasn't sure you could," Hope said tartly, "considering the way you were looking at those women."

Cody laughed. "Me? What about Eli? And besides, there was only one woman in that room who really interested me."

"And who was that?"

"I think you know who."

Hope blushed to the roots of her very blond hair, but she said, "I presume that you mean Rachel Peyton. I can assure you that she's locked securely in her room. Eli and

I saw to that, since you seemed more interested in a walk outside than in the welfare of your prisoners."

"Oh, I'm interested in Rachel, all right," Cody said. "I'm interested in seeing her locked up in the Del Rio jail. But this is another woman I was talking about; I'm interested in her in a whole different way."

"And what way is that?"

For an answer, Cody reached to the other chair and took her hand. There was no resistance as he drew her up and over to where he was sitting, and there was none as he pulled her down to him and kissed her thoroughly.

When the kiss was finished, Hope pushed herself away and stood up. Brushing back a strand of hair that had fallen across her cheek, she said, "You certainly have a direct way of expressing your interest."

"Yes, ma'am, I reckon I do," Cody agreed. "I don't see that there's any reason to pussyfoot around about it."

Hope sat back down in her own chair and took a deep breath. "I believe that we've gotten off the subject, however. We were talking about the Carswells."

Cody sighed. "There's something funny about them, all right," he said, "even if we can't pin it down. I tried to find out from Carswell where they were from and how they happened to be out here in this part of the country, but he wouldn't give me a straight answer to either part of the question."

"None of his daughters said anything about that at dinner, either. Did you notice that they talked only in general terms about their backgrounds? No one ever mentioned a specific place where they'd lived before."

Cody hadn't noticed, probably distracted by their charms—but he didn't think this would be the right time to mention that. "Another thing that bothers me is how Carswell makes a living out here. Eli has a hard time just supporting himself, and that story Rachel told isn't far off the truth for a lot of folks that settle out here. What does Carswell do to support four daughters?"

"Ranching?" Hope suggested.

"Did you see any cattle? He didn't seem too concerned about going out and feeding his herd, if he has one, and this storm would've made feeding a necessity."

"Maybe he has money from . . . investments."

"Maybe," Cody acknowledged, though for some reason he didn't believe it. "Another thing I'd like to know is how he got title to this land and house. I never heard a word in Del Rio about the place being sold. I told him the story about how the place came to be vacant, and I'd swear that he'd never heard it. I don't think he even knew who the former owner was or anything about him until I told him."

"He could have bought the house through the owner's family," Hope said.

"Sure he could, but I don't think it happened that way. I have this real strong sense that no one knows he's living here. I think he just moved in and took over."

"But that brings us back to where we were. Why would he want to be here? He doesn't act like a man who has something to hide."

"He might not act like it, but I'm pretty sure he's hiding something, all right. I just don't know what."

"You're just thinking like a lawman," Hope said. "And even if he is hiding something, it might not be any of our business."

"It might not be our business, but you're just as suspicious as I am," Cody pointed out. "And you're the one who brought it up in the first place. But you're right. Maybe it's none of our business. Anyway, even if it is, it's too late to worry about it tonight." He reached out a hand for her again, but she got up from her chair and moved away.

"I need to think about that awhile before we do it again," she said.

That was fine with Cody. Some things you couldn't rush. He stood up and said, "I'll see you in the morning."

"Yes, in the morning."

Cody went back to his room, whistling under his breath. He was already looking forward to morning when he opened the door and got the biggest surprise of the last several days.

Francesca Carswell was lying in his bed, her red hair spread out on the pillow, her green eyes sparkling with mischief.

As Cody stood there watching, the eldest of the Carswell daughters sat up and let the covers slip away from her shoulders. From what Cody could see, she wasn't wearing a stitch of clothing, and the sight of her breasts stopped him in his tracks. They were firm and high, with dark aureoles and long, erect nipples that appeared to Cody to be pointing straight at him.

"Good evening, Mr. Cody," Francesca said. "I've been warming your bed for you."

Cody swallowed hard and stepped into the room, closing the door behind him.

CHAPTER

||||||||||||||||||||||||| **7** |||||||||||||||||||||||||

The stars shone like points of ice in the black night sky, and the moon was a pale ghost among the thin clouds.

The Reverend Liam Woodley saw no beauty in the sight, however. He was lost, irretrievably lost. There was such a sameness to the landscape by both day and night that he was no longer certain he would recognize the trail he'd been looking for even if he ran across it, and nothing short of a miracle from God was going to save him and those under his care.

"What do you think, Preacher?" the man sitting beside him on the wagon seat said. "Don't you reckon we better give it a rest for the night and see if we can't make a fresh start in the morning?"

Both men were wearing thick coats and gloves, and they were wrapped in blankets as well. When they spoke, their breath frosted the air in front of them.

"I suppose that we might as well, Brother Forbes," Woodley said.

His voice, even when he pitched it low, carried for a great distance. Like Captain Wallace Vickery, Woodley could preach hell hot and heaven high and fill any building with his booming sermons. His appearance belied the voice, however. He was a man in his late fifties, no more than an inch or two over five feet, and under his hat there was very little hair to warm his nearly bald head, only a few tufts of white that clung to the back and sides. He had a weathered look, like that of a man who had spent much of his life in harsh conditions, but he had never experienced anything quite like the storm that had caught him and his fellow pilgrims unawares the previous evening.

"Pull in behind those rocks," he told Josiah Forbes, pointing off to the left. "They'll give us a little bit of shelter in case the wind comes up again."

Forbes clucked to the mules, and they pulled the wagon toward the rocks. Their hooves slipped occasionally, but they were getting better at walking on the glassy ice, though they still had a little trouble when the wagon wheels slipped.

The Reverend Woodley glanced at Forbes, who was a deacon in the Pandale Baptist Church—the church that Woodley served—and the richest man in the small frontier town, the owner of the general store. He had left his wife and seven children behind to attend a religious revival meeting in Del Rio with Woodley and several others. The preacher had often suspected that Forbes's convictions were something less than he professed them to be, and he'd been somewhat surprised when the merchant expressed a desire to be part of the small group going to the revival. Woodley thought perhaps it was just an excuse for Forbes to get away from his large family, for whom he seemed to have no great affection.

As the wagon moved toward the unpromising shelter of the rocks, Woodley looked back over his shoulder. Following behind them in a second wagon were the Evanses, William and Nancy, and Kenneth and Sue Beth Prescott, all members of Woodley's congregation, all on their way to the revival.

And all of them Woodley's responsibility.

They were relatively young, none of them yet in their thirties, and none of them had ever experienced hardships that even came close to what they had gone through in the last twenty-four hours. William Evans was the telegrapher on a Southern Pacific railroad spur line, while Kenneth Prescott owned and operated a hardware store that was just beginning to produce a profit. Both wives were devoted to their husbands, and both were childless, which Woodley thought was a good thing, considering the circumstances.

Caring for a child would have been a real problem in the bone-chilling cold.

After the wagons were stopped and the mules had been unhitched, Forbes addressed the group. "We're in a hell of a mess, folks. You'll have to pardon my language, Preacher, ladies, but it's the truth. Old Scratch couldn't have planned it any better if he were runnin' things himself. We're out of food, we're out of water, and we don't have any wood for a fire. I'd like to know if there's gonna be manna from heaven, and if there's not, what're we gonna do?"

Woodley listened to the speech with Christian patience. The fact that they were without food was no one's fault. They should have been in Del Rio before nightfall the previous day, and they would have been if a spoke hadn't broken in a wheel of the wagon William Evans was driving. By the time they'd gotten it repaired, it was almost dark, and they had been on the road for less than an hour afterward when the storm had caught them.

The lack of wood was perhaps Woodley's fault. They had camped the previous night in a grove of trees, where there'd been plenty of dead wood to burn. Woodley hadn't thought to take any of it along since he believed that they'd easily find the trail again and get to Del Rio before dark. But they hadn't found the trail, and Woodley blamed himself for the lack of kindling—though no one else had thought about bringing it with them, either.

"We have blankets," he said. "We can nestle together for warmth. Surely by tomorrow the ice will melt and we can find the trail again."

They were lucky to have blankets, he thought. They were carrying the bedrolls in case they had to provide their own accommodations in Del Rio.

"What if we don't find the trail?" Forbes asked. His usually florid face looked pale and spectral in the moonlight. "What then?"

"*Jehovah jireh,*" Woodley said. "The Lord will provide."

"I'd feel a hell of a lot better—'scuse me again, ladies, Preacher—if He'd provide me with a big steak right about now," Forbes said. "Or even a piece of bread. Or a fire."

"We can have a fire," William Evans said.

"How's that?" Forbes asked.

"We can break up part of one of the wagon beds," Kenneth Prescott said. "William and I talked about it a while ago. I've got a knife to make some shavings with, and we can start a fire. Those planks in the wagon beds'll burn just fine, and the rocks'll absorb some of the heat, hold it in, and help keep us warm. We can melt some ice, and then we'll have water to drink. We'll be all right. Just hungry, that's all."

"That's all well and good, I reckon," Forbes said, still clearly not satisfied. "But what about tomorrow?"

William Evans smiled. *"Jehovah jireh,"* he said.

Unfortunately, he sounded no more convincing than Woodley had.

Cody was only human, and the sight of a beautiful, naked woman was naturally quite arousing. At the same time he felt vaguely uneasy with the thought that this was the daughter of his host. There was such a thing as carrying hospitality too far.

"You shouldn't be here," he said.

Francesca cocked her head. "Why not? It's my house. I can go where I want to." She made no move to cover herself.

Cody felt ridiculous, practically at a loss for words. He thought it was a lot easier to deal with a band of marauding outlaws than with a single naked woman.

"What I meant was, you shouldn't be here . . . like that."

Francesca looked down at herself. "Is there something wrong with me?"

"There's nothing wrong with you," Cody said, swallowing again. No, there certainly wasn't anything wrong with her. He could hardly look away.

"Then why don't you come over here and join me?" Francesca asked, patting the sheets beside her. "The bed's nice and warm already, and I think the two of us could warm it up even more."

Cody was still standing near the door. "I don't think that would be a good idea."

Francesca didn't agree. "It seems like a fine idea to me," she told him.

"Your father—"

"Won't know a thing about it. I'm not going to tell him. Are you?"

"No. But—"

She grinned. "Then let's stop talking. There are other things that are so much more interesting."

Cody knew that had the situation been different, he wouldn't have shown the same restraint. But his recent visit to Hope's room had convinced him that her feelings for him were as strong as his were for her. He was not ready to betray those feelings for a casual encounter with Francesca, no matter how strongly he was tempted or how willing she seemed.

"Come on," Francesca teased, apparently taking his hesitation for shyness, "there's nothing to be afraid of. I won't bite you. Unless, of course, you want me to."

"I'm not afraid," Cody said. "I just don't think it'd be right. I'm going to have to ask you to leave."

"Leave?" Francesca was incredulous. "You don't really mean that."

"I sure do," Cody said. He had a sudden inspiration and put a hand to his bandage. "Fact is, the doctor tells me that I have a concussion. I'm not up to any strenuous activity."

"Oh, I guarantee you it would be strenuous," Francesca said. She threw aside the covers and got out of the bed, letting Cody have a good look at what he would be missing. "Are you sure you won't change your mind? It might be worth the risk."

Cody's mouth was dry. "It might. But I better not."

Francesca reached for a green robe that was hanging on the nearest bedpost. "Someday you're going to be sorry that you turned me down."

Watching her slip on the robe—which she took her time getting into—Cody was already sorry.

"It's not because of some silly Ranger vow you took, is it?" Francesca asked as she belted the robe. "If it is, I'm not sure that Ranger vows even count when you get this far out in the country."

"It's not a vow," Cody said. "It's me."

"That's too bad, then." Francesca walked by him and put her hand on the doorknob. He could smell her perfume. "For both of us."

She opened the door and went out, closing it gently behind her.

Cody let out a sigh. He wondered what he would have done if he hadn't met Hope or if she'd stayed back in Del Rio. He didn't have to wonder long. He was damn sure he'd have been in bed with that long-legged redhead right now. He sighed again.

But there was no use thinking about missed opportunities. Taking off his shirt, he walked over to the nightstand and poured water from the pitcher into the washbowl. It was good and cold. Just what he needed. He splashed it on his face just as he heard the door open behind him.

Francesca was more persistent than he thought she'd be. He grabbed a towel and started drying his face to get the water out of his eyes.

But when he turned around, it wasn't Francesca he saw. It was Diana, the auburn-haired daughter who had first appeared in his room earlier that day, the one who had gone for her father.

She wasn't naked, but she was dressed in a robe much like the one Francesca had put on, except that this one was red. And it was obvious that she was wearing nothing underneath it.

This is the damnedest house I've ever been in, Cody told himself. He stood there speechless, holding the towel, his mouth open.

Diana didn't mind his silence. She walked over to the bed and looked down. "Someone's been sleeping in your bed," she said.

"Uh," Cody managed to say. He didn't know whether to mention Francesca or not. Did Diana know that her sister had just left the room only a minute or two before?

Diana put a hand on the sheets. "Warm," she said. "I like it that way."

She untied the belt of her robe and shrugged the garment from her shoulders.

"Wait!" Cody yelped, tossing the towel to the washstand.

Diana turned to face him, the robe hanging half off her shoulders. "Wait for what?"

A good question, Cody thought, eyeing her breasts. They were larger than Francesca's, with wide, stubby nipples.

"I, uh, have a head injury," he said, using the excuse that had persuaded Francesca to leave.

"I'm not interested in your *head*," Diana said, taking a step toward him.

Cody looked around for his shirt, but before he could reach it, Diana had stepped up and pressed herself against him. The stiffened nipples of her soft breasts seemed to burn his chest like hot coals.

She ran her hand down his chest to the front of his jeans. "That's not your head I feel, is it?"

Cody backed away. "I have a concussion. Standing up like this makes me dizzy."

"I don't think you're getting dizzy from standing up," Diana said. "I think it's because of something else." She let the robe slip lower.

Cody moved backward until he came to the door. He reached behind him and felt the doorknob. He turned it and opened the door. "No matter why I'm dizzy, I'm just not ready for what you're offering." He had to grin. "Not that it doesn't look good."

"I'm glad you think so, but I wish you'd let me stay."

"I can't," Cody insisted.

Diana shrugged herself back into the robe, making her breasts do interesting things in the process. She pulled the garment around her, never taking her eyes off Cody.

"You're sure about that? About not letting me stay?"

Cody nodded. He was afraid that if he spoke again, he might change his mind. A man's willpower lasted just so long.

Diana looked at him speculatively. "Did you know that some women like the men who turn them down more than they like the men who accept them?"

"I never thought of that," Cody said.

"Well, it's true." She touched Cody on the bicep as she left the room. "Think about that."

Cody was sure that he would.

There were no more interruptions, and Cody was finally able to blow out the lamp and go to bed. But he wasn't able to fall asleep immediately. He was too bothered by the unconventional behavior of the Carswell sisters, which seemed to reinforce his and Hope's feeling that there was something strange about the family.

It wasn't that no woman had ever offered herself to Cody before, but none had done so in such a blatant fashion, and there had certainly never been two women throwing themselves at him in such a short space of time. Cody had no false modesty; he knew that many women found him attractive. But it was still an unusual experience to have two naked women in his room in the same evening.

And it was even more unusual that he had turned both of them down. Marie Jermaine would never have believed it, had he told her about it—which, of course, he had no intention of doing. He didn't think he'd mention it to Hope, either, though she was the main reason the women had been rejected. There was no point in making her too sure of herself.

Just before he drifted off, Cody remembered that he hadn't checked on Gus all day. He'd have to do that first thing tomorrow, he told himself. And then he was dreaming of sunshine and summertime.

It was the giggles that woke him up, though Cody later thought that he must have been sleeping pretty deeply not to have felt something when the two women got into bed with him.

Because that was the situation he found himself in when he came fully awake: sandwiched between the two youngest Carswell daughters, Brenna and Phoebe, both of them giggling, both of them buck naked.

For a moment or two Cody thought that he must still be dreaming. There was no way what was happening to him could be real. But he soon discovered that it was, when he was almost smothered in breasts, thighs, and Brenna's long hair as the two young women rubbed their bodies against him with abandon. It wasn't an unpleasant sensation, he had to admit, and he was sorry that he had to call it to a halt.

He sat up and pushed them off to the sides of the bed. One of them had lit the lamp, though the wick was turned down, and he could see that they lacked none of the enticing curves of their older sisters.

"What's the matter?" Phoebe asked. "Did we wake you up?"

Brenna pushed her disheveled hair out of her face. "If we did, that's exactly what we wanted to do. You wouldn't be much good to us if you were asleep."

Cody felt trapped between the two of them, but he didn't want to try climbing over either one. There was no telling what they might grab hold of to keep him there.

"What's the matter?" Phoebe repeated. "Are you shy? There's no need to be. And we're twice as much fun as Diana."

"Or Francesca," Brenna said. She reached out for Cody's hands and put them on her breasts. "Ohhhhh, your hands are cold. See if he's cold all over, Phoebe."

Phoebe dived under the covers, her smoothly rounded rump sticking out.

"No, he's not cold all over at all, Brenna," her muffled voice said. "He's *real* warm down here."

Things had gone too far. Cody threw himself to the side and twisted out of the bed, landing on the cold floor. He jumped up and grabbed his pants, pulling them on as he hopped from one foot to the other.

"I want you two to get up and get out of that bed," he said, trying to sound angrier than he actually felt. "It's late and I don't feel well and I want some sleep."

"I don't think he likes us, Phoebe," Brenna said with a pout. "What do you think?"

"He's real mean, all right," her sister replied as she emerged from beneath the covers. "My feelings are hurt."

"Mine, too," Brenna agreed. "What do you think we should do about it?"

Cody grinned in spite of himself. "I don't think either

one of you's had her feelings hurt in years." He saw their robes hanging on opposite bedposts and took one in each hand. He tossed them over. "Now, put these on like good little girls and go to your own rooms. I've had a hard day, and I need some rest."

"You're sure going to be lonesome in this big old bed if we leave," Phoebe warned.

"I know that," Cody said. "And it's not that I don't appreciate your offer. But I think you better put on those robes."

Phoebe looked at Brenna. "He's sure not much fun, is he?"

Brenna sighed. "Not a bit." She began slipping into the robe. "But we knew that, didn't we?"

"But we're a lot of fun. Much more fun than our sisters." Phoebe pouted. "I don't see how he can treat us this way."

"Believe me, it's not easy," Cody said truthfully. "But I really do need some sleep."

"You can sleep when you're dead," Brenna said. "But there's lots of other things you can't do."

"That's right," Phoebe said, "and one of 'em's—"

"I know, I know," Cody interrupted. "But I'm not planning to be dead for a long time."

"Does that mean we can come back tomorrow night?" Phoebe asked.

"By tomorrow night, I'll be in Del Rio," Cody said.

"I wouldn't count on that," Brenna said. "It might be frozen over for a long time. A real long time."

"Then we'll just have to wait and see," Cody said. Both of the women had their robes on now. "Are you two about ready to leave?"

"We're not ready," Phoebe said, sliding out of the bed. "But we'll go if you want us to."

"I want you to," Cody said, though he questioned if he really did. Two women like that didn't drop into your bed every night of the year. Or any night of your life, he thought.

"Good night, then," Phoebe said, going through the door.

"Sleep tight," Brenna said, as she closed the door behind them.

Cody wondered if he'd be able to sleep at all, but he knew one thing for sure. It wasn't even morning yet, and he'd already had a night he would never forget.

CHAPTER
8

The next day dawned gray and cold. The sun that had appeared the previous day was hidden behind gray clouds so heavy and low that the Reverend Woodley thought he might be able to reach up and touch them if he were only a foot or two taller. He looked all around. Except for the pile of rocks, the land was as featureless as ever.

Like Cody, Liam Woodley and his small group of pilgrims had spent a night that they would never forget, but theirs had been memorable for other reasons—reasons that had a lot more to do with hunger and cold than with the hymns that Woodley had led them in or the prayers that he had so earnestly sent up to heaven.

Woodley wondered now about the efficacy of those prayers. It appeared that they must have stopped somewhere about the level of the clouds rather than ascending all the way to heaven, for he had prayed mightily and at length for their deliverance from the prison of ice that surrounded them and kept them from their destination—and deliverance hadn't arrived. If anything, the day promised to be even colder than the one before. The dome of arctic air that had settled over them was as immobile as one of the large rocks they had spent the night beside.

Josiah Forbes, never at a loss for words, expressed his feelings as he helped Evans and Prescott hitch the mules to the wagons. "You know we're not gonna make it, don't you, Preacher? You know we're gonna freeze to death out here, miles away from anywhere and anybody."

Woodley looked at the women. He didn't like such talk in front of them. Men could understand and accept such things, but women had to be protected from them.

"The Lord will take care us, Brother Forbes," he said. "In the words of the psalmist, 'Yea, though I walk through the valley of the shadow of Death—' "

"This is no valley, and there aren't any shadows that I see," Forbes cut in. "And I don't see any green pastures, either. All I can see is a bunch of ice and snow, so you might as well give up on the Scriptures, Preacher."

He looked around and waved a hand at the desolate landscape. "I don't even know that it's worth goin' on. We might as well sit here and wait for what's comin'. At least we could have a fire until we used the wagons up. And we could eat one of the mules. There'd be plenty of meat to last until the thaw comes, and then we could find our way home. That way we'd have a chance."

"Surely you don't mean that, Mr. Forbes," Sue Beth Prescott said. "These poor dumb animals deserve better from us than that."

"A cow's a poor dumb animal," Forbes said. "And I wouldn't turn down a steak right now, would you? Another thing, we've just been lucky so far that one of these mules hasn't slipped and broke its leg. What're we gonna do then? Just shoot it and leave it?"

"We must have faith that things will work together for good, Brother Forbes," Woodley said. "The Lord works in mysterious ways, and He may have sent us on this journey for a purpose. It's up to us to discover what that purpose is."

"The purpose might be for us to freeze to death," Forbes muttered. "Did you ever think of that, Preacher?"

Forbes was confirming everything Woodley had ever thought about the limits of the deacon's faith, but the minister did not chide him for that. He said, "If that's the Lord's purpose, then we'll just have to carry it out as bravely as we can, Brother Forbes."

Evans and Prescott didn't look too happy at that comment, but they went on hitching up the teams. Woodley was glad to see that they were made of sterner stuff than Forbes, who had been a deacon in the church long before

Woodley had ever come to Pandale. The preacher wondered briefly how Forbes had ever attained the position, which implied a certain amount of honor and character.

"I just want you to know that I'm holding you responsible for whatever happens to us, Preacher," Forbes said. "When we're standing there at the Pearly Gates, you'd better have a good explanation."

Woodley thought, somewhat uncharitably, that in the event of Brother Forbes's death the deacon might be standing at an entirely different location, but he didn't put the thought into words. Instead, he turned and looked out at the field of ice and said a silent prayer for their safe arrival at the end of their journey.

The fire had died and the room was cold. Cody hated to get out from under the quilts that covered him, but he wanted to glance out the window and get a look at the day, to see if he was going to be able to take his prisoners in. As cold as it was in the room, it would be much colder outside, so the Ranger was pessimistic about his chances of getting started on the trip. Gus and Eli probably weren't up to it, and nothing had been done yet about the wrecked buggy.

He shivered as he pulled on his pants and shirt and socks; then he slipped his feet into his cold boots and walked over to the window. He moved the curtain aside and looked out.

What he saw did nothing to cheer him up. Icicles still hung from the roof, ice still covered the ground for as far as he could see, and the sky was a uniform dull gray. He let the curtain drop.

There was no wood on the hearth, so Cody was about to go looking for some when there was a knock on the door. He was almost afraid to open it—but surely the four Carswell daughters wouldn't be trying anything in the daytime.

He opened the door cautiously. It was Hope. Relieved, he opened it wider so that she could come in.

"Good morning," she said. She looked fresh and pretty, and Cody found that he was quite pleased with himself for having resisted last night's temptations.

"Morning," he said. "I wonder if they're going to serve us breakfast."

"They certainly served us a fine dinner," Hope said. "So I expect they'll have breakfast as well. Why don't we go down and find out?"

"Good idea," Cody agreed.

He wondered whether he should tell her about what had happened to him the previous night. His first thought was that he shouldn't, but then he thought that if he didn't she might find out some other way—from one of the sisters, for example. Cody wouldn't put it past them to tell the story and maybe make more of it than there really was.

Besides, it was possible that Hope had seen or heard something. Her room was near his, and she might just be waiting for him to give her an explanation.

"There's something I need to tell you before we go downstairs," Cody began.

"There's something I wanted to talk to you about, too," Hope said. "But you can go first."

Cody quickly told her about the sisters' visits to his room, glossing over most of the intimate details but telling enough to make it clear that their intentions had been carnal in the extreme.

Hope didn't seem nearly as shocked as Cody thought she'd be. He found out the reason.

"I thought it might be something like that," Hope said. "You see, I had a visitor last night as well."

"What! Who?"

Hope was blushing. "Hayden Carswell."

"That old son of a bitch," Cody said, his hand going to the butt of the Colt. "I'll kill him."

Hope didn't chide Cody for his language. "There's no need for anything quite so drastic. It's not that I don't appreciate the thought, though. It shows that you really do care for me. But I wouldn't want you to think that I'm not capable of handling something like that. I'm perfectly capable."

"*You're* going to kill him?"

Hope laughed. "Of course not. Heavens, I wish you could see the expression on your face. What I meant was, there are other ways to take care of that kind of situation."

"I'd like to know what they are."

"Well, first of all, you should know that he wasn't nearly as blatant as his daughters seem to have been. But maybe you were exaggerating."

Cody shook his head. "Believe me, I wasn't exaggerating. I was being decorous, if anything."

Hope gave him an arch look. "Then maybe *I'm* the one who should be jealous."

"I told you, nothing happened," Cody said. "And who said anything about being jealous?"

Hope smiled sweetly. "I was only making a joke. At any rate, Carswell didn't disrobe or anything quite so vulgar. He came to the door to ask if I was comfortable, or so he said. Then he asked to come in. I didn't see any harm in that, and at first there wasn't. He just talked a little about his family and how proud he was of his daughters."

"But not for long," Cody guessed.

"You're right. It didn't take him long to get around to telling me that I'd been on his mind since dinner and that he hadn't seen a woman so pretty since his wife died."

"And you're still sure you don't want me to kill him?" Cody asked.

"Of course. I don't mind a compliment. But I could tell he was really implying something else, something not nearly so simple as flirtation."

"So what did you do?"

"I told him that I was flattered and that he reminded me of someone, too."

"And who was that?"

"My grandfather," Hope said, laughing. "He didn't stay around for long after that."

Cody laughed, too. "I don't blame him. He strikes me as the kind of fella who has a pretty high opinion of himself. I reckon you took him down a peg or two."

"I should hope so. I don't think he'll be back." Her eyes narrowed. "But I'm not so sure I can say the same about those four daughters of his."

"You don't have to worry about them," Cody told her. "I made it pretty clear that I wasn't interested in what they were peddling. But I'm not as sure about Carswell as you are. I don't see him as the type who discourages easy."

"Maybe he'd be back to see me if the circumstances were different," Hope said. "As it is, I think he found his comfort elsewhere."

"Rachel," Cody said disgustedly. "You're talking about Rachel."

"That's right. I heard him knocking on her door almost as soon as he left my room. I didn't go to sleep for about an hour, but I never did hear him come out."

Cody didn't like hearing that at all. There was no telling what Rachel might have told Carswell or what the two of them might have cooked up between themselves.

He said, "I'd like to get away from this place, and the sooner we can leave, the better I'll like it. What about Gus? Can he travel yet?"

"I haven't looked in on him today. Perhaps we should do that."

"Let's go," Cody said, propelling her out of the room. "And while we're at it, let's check on Eli, too."

They stopped at Eli's room first. The rancher was up and dressed, and he appeared to be feeling fine. He unbuttoned his shirt so that Hope could check his dressing.

"It looks good," she said. "No sign of bleeding. Are you feeling all right?"

"Right as rain," Eli assured her as he rebuttoned the shirt. "I'll be as good as new 'fore you know it."

"What about traveling?" Cody asked. "If we can borrow a buggy or wagon from Carswell, could you make it to Del Rio today?"

Eli looked thoughtful. "Well, now, I sort of had it in mind not to go into Del Rio with you—that is, if you didn't mind. I thought it might be all right for me to stay here for a while. Maybe get a little better acquainted with these folks, since they're practically my neighbors, you might say."

Cody had found that same idea amusing when he'd thought of it at dinner last evening, but it didn't have the same appeal to him now. "I think you better come with us, Eli," he said. "There's something funny going on in this house, and I don't like the way things are shaping up here. I don't think it'd be a good idea for you to stay."

Eli looked at him uncomprehendingly. "Why not? They all seem like mighty nice folks."

Cody didn't want to go into the whole story with Eli, but he told him about Carswell's late-night visit to Rachel.

"You don't mean he—" Eli stopped himself and looked at Hope. Then he started over. "You don't mean he had his way with her, do you?"

"That's exactly what I mean," Cody said.

"Good Lord. But she's . . . she's . . . ."

"She's big trouble. That's what she is."

"What're we goin' to do about it?" Eli asked.

"I'm not sure yet," Cody replied. "First, we're going to look in on your brother."

"What then?"

"That depends on how he's doing."

Gus wasn't doing worth a damn, and it didn't take a doctor to see it. His face was drawn and pale, and he didn't even have the energy to raise his head from the pillow to look at them.

He did, however, have enough strength to curse Cody effectively from his prone position.

"Goddamn Texas Rangers," he said, his voice strained. "You goddamn bastard, why didn't you just go ahead and kill me back at Eli's place? It'd be better'n lyin' here waitin' to die."

"Is he goin' to die?" Eli asked.

Hope examined the wound. "I can't say. I'd hoped that he'd be gaining strength by now, and I still think he'll be fine. It just might take a little longer than I thought."

"To hell with that," Gus snarled. "Where's Rachel? Even my own goddamn wife won't come to see me, and I'm a dyin' man."

"You're not dying," Cody said, ignoring the mention of Rachel. "I still plan to take you to Del Rio and see to it that you go to trial. I expect that you'll live long enough to be a guest in the state prison for quite a few years."

"Just like a goddamn lawman," Gus said disgustedly. "Can't let a man die in peace."

"You just need something to eat and drink," Hope said. "Then you'll feel much better. I'll see that something is brought in."

"I want to see Rachel. Where's my wife?"

Hope looked at Cody.

"She's locked in her room," the Ranger said. "I'll see if she wants to come in for a visit later."

"She damn well better. I'm her husband."

Maybe the outlaw really cared for her, Cody thought, but he wasn't so sure the feeling was mutual. Rachel had been willing to take a few risks at Eli's cabin, but she might have found herself a new ally now.

"I'll tell her," Cody said. "Right now, we need to see about something to eat for all of us. Somebody'll bring you a tray."

Gus didn't answer. He turned his face away and didn't even look at them as they left the room.

There had been nothing more solid than water in William Evans's stomach for so long that he felt all that was left was a hard knot where his belly had once been, and the hunger made the cold even worse.

His toes and fingers were so cold they were numb, and he was afraid that if he accidentally knocked them against the side of the wagon they might just drop off, like an icicle might drop off the eave of a house if you tapped it with a hammer. Even his eyeballs were cold, and he found it easier and easier just to leave his eyes closed every time he blinked.

But he told himself that he couldn't close his eyes. He was the one driving the wagon, and he figured he had about another half hour before it'd be Prescott's turn.

He wished Josiah Forbes hadn't been quite so blunt about what their chances were. It wasn't that he was worried for himself; he'd lived a Christian life, and although he'd made his share of mistakes, he thought he was as likely as anyone to wind up facing those Pearly Gates that Forbes had mentioned. Nancy and Sue Beth would surely wind up there, too, but somehow it didn't seem right for two such devout women to be going through the same trials that the four men were. Women were strong in the faith. Evans had no doubt of that. But everyone knew they weren't as able to stand physical hardship as men were.

Still, Evans told himself, the preacher always said that God never gave folks a trial they couldn't endure. Evans was awfully tired, though, and he didn't know how much longer he was going to be able to endure this particular trial. He didn't think any of them would make it through the day, much less the terrible night that was sure to follow.

He swayed slightly in the wagon seat and then jerked upright, realizing that he had almost gone to sleep. It would be so easy to sleep, he thought. Then he'd no longer feel the biting cold that seemed to have somehow eaten its way past his clothing and even his skin and entered his whole body, which now was nothing but a hollow shell filled with icy, aching cold.

As he tried to sit straighter in the seat he looked out across the plains. What he saw was ice, ice, and more ice. There was no sign of a trail or a road, no sign of anything. They were never going to find their way to Del Rio. They were going to die right here, and come springtime maybe some wandering rider would find their wagons and their bones.

He looked over at the other wagon. The Reverend Woodley slumped in the seat beside Deacon Forbes, who was driving the team. Evans wondered if Woodley was asleep or praying, though he was beginning to think that prayer wasn't going to do them any good. He'd never doubted prayer before, but he was doubting it now, and he knew that was a bad sign.

God will provide, he told himself. But he wondered just exactly *what* God was going to provide. If they could only come across a house, even a deserted house, he'd be happy.

And that was when he saw something sticking up on the horizon, something that looked like maybe a rock, a gigantic rock, all alone on the icy fields.

He'd never heard tell of a rock that big, but that didn't mean there couldn't be one, of course. He stared at it harder. They weren't going straight on toward the rock, but Evans kept watching it as the wagon moved aimlessly along. The more he looked, the less it looked like a rock.

In fact, it was a house.

"A house!" he shouted. "It's a house!"

The others roused up and looked where he was pointing. Forbes, in the other wagon, was visibly excited.

Woodley's voice boomed across the plains. "Thank you, Jesus, for you have delivered us!"

They turned the wagons and headed toward the distant structure. Knowing what they had been delivered from, they never stopped to wonder what they were being delivered into.

CHAPTER
||||||||||||||||||||||||| **9** |||||||||||||||||||||||||||

Cody saw them first.

He was in Gus's room, watching Brenna trying to feed the outlaw from a plate of scrambled eggs and bacon, but Gus was so weak and dispirited that he couldn't—or wouldn't—even take a bite. He had turned his face to the wall at Brenna's first attempt, and no amount of coaxing could persuade him to turn back.

Brenna, and the other three sisters for that matter, had surprised Cody at breakfast by their complete nonchalance. They'd sat at the table, laughing and talking and eating as if nothing unusual had occurred in Cody's bedroom, and their friendliness to him and Hope and Eli had been totally unforced. If they felt rebuffed in any way, they were experts at hiding their feelings.

Hayden Carswell, dressed much as he had been the day before, had sat at the head of the table being the perfect host. He'd even had the effrontery to ask Hope if she had passed a pleasant night. Hope had put her hand on Cody's knee under the table to restrain him, so Cody hadn't called Carswell on it. Rachel had been there, too, and there was something decidedly different about her. Cody would have noticed it even if Hope hadn't told him of her suspicions. Rachel had been smiling and animated, even joining in the conversation occasionally. She had eaten heartily, but Cody had noted that she spent a great deal of her time looking at Carswell when she thought no one was watching her.

Cody had wondered if the two of them had enjoyed just a romp in bed or if there was more to it. It wasn't impossible that they had cooked something up, something that would make his job even harder. Rachel was going to bear watching even more closely than before.

After they'd eaten, Cody asked about fixing a plate for Gus. Brenna had volunteered to do it and to take the food to the room. She'd even said she wouldn't mind feeding him.

Cody hadn't tried to stop her, but he knew that he'd have to be in the room with her. Although Gus was wounded and weak, he wasn't to be trusted alone in the room with a young woman like Brenna.

But Gus didn't try anything, and neither did Brenna, though Cody was afraid that she might want to take advantage of their being together to repeat her performance of the night before. She kept her distance, however, and Cody found that he wasn't nearly as uncomfortable around her as he'd expected to be. In fact, he found himself enjoying her high spirits as she tried to josh Gus into eating some of the scrambled eggs she'd made.

"Oh, come on now, you stubborn old mule," she said. "Take a bite for me. You wouldn't want to insult my cooking, would you?"

Gus didn't say a word. He just lay there and looked at the wall.

"I don't think he's going to give in," Cody said.

Brenna looked up from where she was sitting on the bed. "He might. Not everybody turns down something that they'd enjoy if they just gave it a try."

Cody didn't know what to say to that, so he didn't say anything. He walked over to the window, moved the curtain aside, and looked out.

And spotted something moving across the ice toward the house.

"What on earth?" he muttered, half to himself.

Brenna heard him, though, because in a second she was at his side, gazing out.

"It's somebody in wagons," she said. "They're coming this way."

They were coming very slowly and carefully, the mules putting their feet down warily on the slick ice.

"I'd better get downstairs and see who it is," Cody said.

"You can keep on trying to get Gus to eat, if you don't mind."

"I do mind," Brenna said. "It's not often that we get two bunches of visitors at the same time. I'm going down, too."

There wasn't any way Cody could stop her; he didn't have any authority over her, and he couldn't order her to keep trying to feed Gus. He wished that Gus would eat. The outlaw needed to get his strength back for the trip to Del Rio. But maybe those wagons offered a way to get to town no matter how bad Gus was feeling.

On the other hand, what if the wagons were bringing even more trouble? Cody didn't think that was likely, but it was something he had to check out.

He turned from the window to advise Brenna to be cautious, but she was already gone. He could hear her in the hallway, calling for her father and sisters.

By the time Cody got downstairs, the whole Carswell clan was on the porch. Hope was there, too, along with Eli. They were all staring at the spectacle of the two wagons that came slipping and sliding into the yard.

One of the men in the wagons was praising the Lord in a resonant voice.

"Hallelujah!" the small man in the dark suit said. "Thank you, Jesus! You have led us safe from our wanderings, and we give you the glory and the praise for it all!" The other travelers seemed more interested in getting out of the wagons and into the house than in listening to the preacher's outpouring of gratitude.

The burly man driving the lead wagon was the first one to touch ground, and he was in such a hurry that he immediately lost his footing and fell sprawling by the wagon. But he got to his feet without help and was on his way to the porch before the others could come to his aid. He didn't stop to say a word to those gathered on the porch; he simply pushed through them and went into the house.

The dark-suited man who was obviously a preacher reached the porch and introduced himself and the rest of the "little flock," as he called them. "I'll ask your pardon for Brother Forbes. We've all suffered quite a bit from the cold, and he's just looking for warmth."

"You're welcome to shelter here," Hayden Carswell said. "There's plenty of room for everyone. Let's all go inside, and you can tell us your story."

The story had to wait, however, because the moment everyone stepped inside, Forbes appealed for something he considered much more urgent.

"Food!" he said. "Do you have anything to eat? We haven't had any food in days!"

"It hasn't been that long," Reverend Woodley protested, but Francesca was already leading her sisters into the kitchen.

"The stove's still hot," she said. "Breakfast will be served as soon as we can get it cooked."

"Praise Jesus!" Woodley said. "It's a heaven-sent miracle, no less than a heaven-sent miracle! I can't speak for the others, but I have to confess that even my own faith has just been sorely tested. But now that we've come to a safe haven, I know that the man of faith is rewarded for his patience. I want you to know, Mr. Carswell, that you are laying up for yourself treasures in heaven by giving strangers such as ourselves shelter from the storm. As our Savior said, 'Even as ye have done it to the least of these, ye have done it unto me.' "

"You're not the only ones taking shelter here," Cody said. He explained that he was a Texas Ranger and that he and two others had been on their way to Del Rio with a couple of prisoners when the storm trapped them.

Woodley looked around the room. "And where are those prisoners now?"

"They're locked in their rooms," Cody said. "They won't be bothering you."

"Oh, I didn't expect them to be a bother," Woodley said. "It's just that for the last day or so I've been wondering what God's purpose might have been in trapping my little flock in the storm. Could it be that I was meant to come here to bring the word of the Lord to your prisoners? Maybe I should go right now and read them a few appropriate passages from the Good Book." He pulled a worn Bible from somewhere within his coat and waved it in front of Cody's face.

Cody explained that Gus was in no condition to appreciate the Gospel and that Rachel wasn't likely to be the most receptive of audiences. "Besides, I don't want anyone to be alone with them. They're both tricky and dangerous."

"Deacon Forbes will go with me, and Brother Prescott and Brother Evans, too. We're all interested in saving souls if we can."

"We'll see about it later, then," Cody said. "Right now, I think the most important thing is for you to warm up and get some food inside you."

"There's the Gospel, if I ever heard it," Forbes grunted.

Cody didn't think much of Forbes. All the others had thanked Carswell profusely for his offer of shelter. Forbes was too interested in taking care of his own needs, and as soon as possible, to think of anything so basic as gratitude.

"An act of Christian charity is the Gospel in action," Woodley said. "But I would like to minister to the prisoners later if I can."

"Like I said, we'll see about it," Cody told him, not wanting to be deceitful, but already determined not to let Woodley into Gus's room, or Rachel's, either.

Cody didn't mind a little enthusiasm, but a little went a long way. He was saved from having to say more by the entrance of Brenna, who was carrying a platter heaped with sausage and eggs. Even Woodley forgot his desire to see Gus and Rachel in the sudden urge to satisfy more immediate cravings.

Brenna smiled as she served everyone, and she had a cheerful word for all of them. Cody found himself thinking that if there was no thaw that day and if Forbes and Woodley had to spend the night there, the pastor and his deacon might receive nocturnal visits from the Carswell sisters much like the ones Cody had experienced. He smiled to himself, thinking that the women were likely to be rebuffed again, at least by the Reverend Woodley. Cody wasn't so sure about Forbes, who was eating with a prodigious appetite. It might be that his appetite for other physical pleasures was equally large, though he didn't look the type.

But Cody wasn't going to form any judgments about

types. He'd already been fooled by Hope and Rachel, and he sure wouldn't have guessed in a million years that the Carswell sisters were as wanton as they'd turned out to be. It was getting to where a man just didn't know what to think about folks anymore.

Although Cody was restless for the remainder of the day, he realized that it'd be best not to attempt to travel. The story told by Woodley and his "flock" had convinced the Ranger that travel would be hazardous in more ways than one. In addition to the physical dangers, which Woodley's group had been lucky enough to avoid, there were also dangers such as the possibility of losing your way in a landscape that seemed to lack all distinguishing features.

"No roads, no paths, nothing," was the way Kenneth Prescott phrased it when Cody talked the situation over with him. "It wasn't anybody's fault that we got lost. Nobody could tell where we were."

"The mules were all right, though," Cody pointed out.

"A couple of times there we weren't so sure," Prescott said. "One of 'em would slip and nearly fall. It's a good thing that mules are so sure-footed."

There was one other thing working against Cody's plan to leave. It would've required one of the wagons to haul Gus in, and Cody didn't want to ask any of Woodley's group to try going on into Del Rio until they'd had at least a day to recover from the hardships they had undergone. So unless there was a thaw, everyone was going to be stuck at the Carswell place for another day.

And there wasn't a thaw.

Cody went out nearly every hour to check on the ice, hoping that there'd be some sign of warming, but there was none. The cold had that part of Texas in its grip, and it didn't seem likely that it was going to let go anytime soon.

The day wasn't without its entertainments, however. Thwarted by Cody in his desire to minister directly to the prisoners, Reverend Woodley got Hayden Carswell's permission to have what he referred to as a "service of thanksgiving" in the house's huge parlor.

Cody was persuaded to allow Rachel to attend, since there didn't seem much chance of her doing any harm in such a setting and since everyone was there except Gus, who ate a bite or two of lunch but who expressed no interest in leaving his bed for the service.

There was no piano, but Woodley lined out the hymns and encouraged everyone to join in the singing. The Carswell sisters turned out to have good voices, and Phoebe even sang harmony on several tunes. Hayden Carswell, hardly a virtuoso, made up in enthusiasm what he lacked in talent, and before long even Cody found himself joining in.

The inevitable sermon by Woodley wasn't nearly as long or as dull as Cody had feared it might be, and all in all he had to admit that he enjoyed the whole thing, except for the times that he noticed Rachel looking covertly at Hayden Carswell. But as far as Cody could tell, her amorous glances weren't returned, so he didn't let her looking bother him.

In fact, the whole atmosphere was so wholesome that Cody was almost beginning to feel as he had initially: There were far worse places to be trapped by a storm. He had changed that opinion when the sisters tried to seduce him, but now he believed that things were bound to go smoothly. How could they try anything so dissolute after a religious service? He thought that even as brazen as they were, they'd have to hesitate now.

All he had to do was get through one more night. After all, he asked himself, what else could happen?

He found the answer to that question just after dinner, when he went with Hope to check on Gus and to bring him some of the excellent steak and potatoes they'd had for dinner. Cody was sure that when Gus smelled the delicious aroma of the steak, the outlaw wouldn't be able to resist eating, no matter how bad he felt.

And that might have been true if Gus had been there to smell it; the trouble was, there was no one in the room. The door was still locked, but Gus was gone.

Cody called everyone together in the parlor to ask if

anyone had seen or heard Gus, but of course no one had—or at least no one admitted it.

Gus had been in the room at lunch, because Cody had gone there, with Diana this time, to feed him. As he had at breakfast, the outlaw had refused to eat or talk, and he'd appeared even more lethargic than he had in the morning. Cody had begun to worry about him, but Hope could find nothing physically wrong with him aside from the gunshot wound, and that was healing normally.

"There could be some internal damage," she had said. "Something that isn't showing up on the outside. But I don't think so. It looks like a clean wound to me. He might just be malingering. Maybe he hopes someone will come along to rescue him."

"I think we've pretty well covered that possibility," Cody had said. "A man like Gus is lucky to have one friend. He had four, but three of them are dead, and the other one's locked up right here. I don't think he's looking for any outside help."

"What about that group that showed up here today?" Hope had asked.

"I think they're just exactly what they look like," Cody had replied. He had grimaced. "But given my record of late, I could be wrong about that. I'll keep a close eye on them."

And he had. The house was so large that there was no way to watch everyone at once, but Cody had seen nearly everyone at one time or another after the service held by Woodley, and he didn't see how any of them would've had time to slip away and help Gus escape. Rachel had been locked in her room after the service, and Cody was certain that she hadn't been out of it since.

So where was Gus? No one was able to come up with an answer.

"Well, he's got to be around here somewhere," Cody told the group assembled in the parlor. "We're going to have to search the house and grounds. He's a dangerous man, and I don't like to think about what he might do if we don't find him."

"He didn't look like he could do much of anything,"

Diana said. "You saw how he wouldn't even eat when I took him that plate of lunch earlier."

"He could've been playing possum," Cody insisted. "We've got to search the house."

Hayden Carswell didn't seem to like the idea much, but he agreed. "My daughters will take the upper floor, although it's closed off, so it's highly doubtful that your prisoner could have gained entry, and I will search the barn. My horses can be high-strung with strangers."

"That's fine, only be careful. I'd advise you to carry a pistol," Cody said. "Mr. Prescott, I'd appreciate it if you, Mr. Evans, and Mr. Forbes would look around on the second floor. Eli, you can help them out."

He added Eli to the group because he wasn't certain how the others might react if they did come upon Gus. They carried firearms, but they didn't look as if they were accustomed to using them. Eli, on the other hand, knew just how dangerous Gus could be, and Cody didn't think he'd hesitate anymore, even though Gus was his brother.

"Dr. Baxter and I will search down here, and in the cellar," Cody went on. "If you run across him, come and get me if there's time. If not, deal with him as best you can. And if nobody finds him, we'll all meet back here in the parlor in half an hour."

"What about me?" Woodley asked. "I'm willing to help out."

Cody wasn't too sure that he wanted a preacher meddling in law business, but he said, "You can help down here. Hope and I could use another pair of eyes. But stick close."

"You won't have to worry about me," Woodley said, but Cody knew that he would anyway.

The search didn't take long, and everyone had returned to the parlor even before the half hour was up. No one had seen any sign of Gus Peyton.

"He couldn't've gotten very far in his condition," Cody said. "If he's not in the house, he's got to be outside. I'm going to search out there. I think the rest of you should stay inside."

There were some mild protests, but no one argued strenuously or long. No one actually wanted to go outside into the frigid night, which promised to be just as cold as the past two had been.

Cody bundled up and went out on the porch, carrying a lantern that Carswell had given him. Hope went with him.

"Be careful," Hope said.

"I intend to," Cody told her. "And I want you to be careful, too. I think someone in that house helped Gus escape, and I don't want you getting hurt."

"Who do you suspect?"

"No one in particular. But somehow that door got unlocked and then locked back up. I'm certain Gus didn't jump down from the second floor, no matter how good he might have gotten to feeling. So you'll have to watch everyone. Especially the Carswells."

"I will," Hope promised. She put her hand to Cody's face. "Come back soon."

"Don't worry. I won't stay out in this weather any longer than I have to. Even if Gus made a run for it, I doubt he got very far."

"He might surprise you."

"He might, but I don't think so. Anyway, even if he doesn't get far, he can still cause plenty of trouble. I don't like the idea of him running around loose."

Hope didn't like the idea much, either. "Do you think he'll try to come back to the house?"

"If he does, Eli can take care of him. I've already talked to him about it."

"I hope you find him," Hope said.

Cody stepped down off the porch. "So do I."

CHAPTER
10

Gus had indeed been feeling much better than anyone knew. He was, in fact, feeling pretty good. His wound hardly bothered him, and that pretty brunette had been sneaking food to him between meals. She'd even paid him a visit in the middle of the night. She hadn't brought food, but she'd done a few other things that had left him a little weak but had perked up his spirits mightily.

He hadn't been able to do much moving around, but she'd moved around plenty for both of them. It didn't even bother Gus that Rachel was locked in the room right next door to them, because from what he could hear through the wall, Rachel was having a pretty good time of her own with somebody or other. He didn't mind. Hell, it didn't bother him that Rachel called herself his wife, but it wasn't like they were really married or anything.

The drunk justice of the peace they'd met in a saloon in Laredo couldn't remember half the ceremony they'd asked him to perform, and he'd never even pronounced them man and wife. There was some doubt as to whether he was even a real justice of the peace, and if he was, it probably didn't matter; all the witnesses were drunk, too, and Gus figured there wasn't a one of 'em who would've been able to remember the wedding the next day. And for damn sure there wasn't any piece of paper making things official. Gus didn't have much of a liking for papers of that nature.

The raven-haired beauty—Brenna, her name was—had told Gus that she'd taken a mighty liking to him, which came as no shock at all to him. He just naturally had a way with women, and once they had a taste of him, they were just about ruined for anybody else. It was just a gift he had.

Brenna was no different from the rest, and she told him that she'd help him get away if that was what he wanted.

That was what he wanted, all right, and he told her that he was going to make out like he was real sick so as to throw everybody off and get them so they weren't expecting him to try anything.

"What about your wife?" Brenna asked. "Are you going to leave her behind?"

Gus wasn't sentimental about it. "Hell, that's her look-out. A man's got to take care of himself first."

So Brenna agreed to smuggle in the food and to come for Gus at the first opportunity that presented itself.

"We'll probably have to wait until after dark," she said. "It might be a good idea if you don't let anyone light your lamp. We wouldn't want the light to draw anybody's attention to this room at the wrong time, even by something as innocent as light spilling from under the door."

That was fine by Gus. He could lie in the dark for a while. He'd done it plenty of times before, and he'd done it in places that were a hell of a lot less comfortable than the bedroom he was in now.

Everyone else was downstairs eating supper when his door opened. Gus wasn't surprised that she'd come for him at that time. It was already dark, and everyone would be too occupied with eating to think about him. He'd heard them laughing and talking as they passed by his room on their way to the stairs. Little did they know that when they came to check on him later, he'd be long gone.

"Is that you, Brenna?" he said when the door was closed. It was so dark in the room that he could barely make out the outline of the shadowy figure crossing toward his bed.

"Shhhhhhh!" the figure said.

"Yeah," Gus whispered. "I'll keep quiet. Just let me get out of this bed."

He swung his legs over the side of the bed and sat up, feeling around for his boots, which he knew were beside the bed somewhere.

Almost at once he sensed that something was wrong, and he stopped feeling for the boots. There was a rank odor in the room, an odor of unwashed flesh that was far different from Brenna's light perfume. "What the hell?" Gus said.

Something swished through the air toward his head. He heard it coming and tried to throw himself aside, but he was too late. A hard object crashed into his temple, and he fell off the bed into a darkness far deeper and blacker than the one that filled the room.

When Gus came to, he wasn't in the house anymore. He could tell that much, but he couldn't tell anything else, except that it was very dark and very cold and he had a throbbing headache.

He tried to put a hand to the place where he'd been hit, but he found that he couldn't. His hands were tied together behind his back.

He tried to sit up, but he couldn't do that, either. His feet were tied as well.

"Goddammit!" he shouted. "You better untie me, you son-of-a-bitch lawman! You can't treat me this way!"

Gus's voice echoed back to him, but there was no other answer.

He tried to calm himself. Then he noticed that he seemed to be lying on a wooden floor and that the floor was colder than it had any right to be. That was when he realized that he was naked. He began yelling again. "Goddamn bastard! I don't know what you're pullin', Ranger, but you'd better stop it and be damn quick about it!"

There was no more answer than there had been the first time. Gus lay still, listening, and after a minute, he thought he heard horses stirring around nearby. He must be in the barn. Maybe he wouldn't freeze to death, but it was damn cold nevertheless. The trouble was, he didn't know what he could do about it.

He lay there for a minute as he tried to think of something to do. Yelling wasn't going to help; he'd figured out that much already. And he didn't think he could get out of the ropes that held him. They were tied tight and hard. He'd already lost most of the feeling in his hands and feet, but he wasn't sure whether that was due to the ropes or the cold.

He tried squirming around on the floor, thinking that he might find something he could use to cut himself free, but he found nothing. All he managed to do was peel a bit of skin off his sides and elbows. He lay quiet again.

A door scraped open.

Gus jerked as if he'd been shot. "Who's there?" he asked, his voice shaky.

No one answered, but a match scratched and flared to life. Gus got a glimpse of broad shoulders and a bearded face in the pale light. It wasn't the Ranger. It was someone Gus had never seen before.

"What the hell's goin' on here?" Gus demanded.

The big man didn't say a word. He lit a lamp that he was carrying and set it on the table.

Gus got his first look at the room he was in. His eyes bugged out, and he started to scream, but the sound was squelched when he was abruptly jerked feet first into the air.

When he was swinging there, he saw Brenna come into the room and join the big man. Even upside down Gus could tell that she was smiling in a way she hadn't smiled when she'd come to his room. It was a smile so filled with evil that Gus, who'd never thought of himself as a model of virtue, knew with the power of genuine revelation he was in the presence of a corruption far more powerful than even he had ever dreamed of.

Brenna pulled something shiny from the folds of her dress.

The last thing Gus ever saw was the blade of a single-edged hunting knife glimmering in the lamplight.

And the last thing he ever heard was the sound of his own screams.

Cody walked around the house a third time, his boots crunching on the ice, looking for any trace of Gus. There were no stars as there'd been when he and Carswell were outside the night before. The heavy overcast blocked out all the light from the sky, and the lantern that Cody held in front of him caused his shadow to dance along behind. There was no sign of Gus, no sign of anyone or anything. The ice was too hard in most places for anyone to make tracks. The mules had broken through here and there, but a man just didn't weigh enough.

The lantern cast a small circle of light around Cody, and he peered into the darkness outside the yellow ring as he looked for any indication that Gus had passed by that way. He had circled the house three times in widening loops without seeing anything of significance.

That didn't mean Gus hadn't made a run for it, but somehow Cody had the feeling that he hadn't gotten very far from the house. After all, where could a man go on a night so dark and cold? It was easy for Cody to understand why Woodley and his flock had been lost for so long.

Cody eyed the barn. Though Hayden Carswell had searched it earlier, if Gus had escaped the house only to discover that travel was impossible, he might have doubled back and taken refuge in the barn, thinking he could hide out in there until morning and then clear out. Besides, there was no place else for him to go. Cody headed for the barn.

After a minute the structure loomed in front of him, and Cody had to put the lantern down to open the barn door. It creaked on its hinges and swung outward as he pulled it.

It was even darker in the barn than it'd been outside, but Cody could hear the animals snuffling and moving around. They seemed to Cody to be jittery, but Carswell had said they tended to be high-strung around strangers. Was he the stranger? he wondered. Or was someone else they weren't used to lurking around nearby?

Cody picked up the lantern and went inside, closing the door behind him. There was something wrong here, all right. He couldn't have explained how he knew, but he did. It was something he sensed, almost like the horses and the mules, he thought.

He checked the stalls, and the fidgety animals jerked away from his touch, though he intended it to be soothing.

He patted his own horse's flank. "That's all right, boy, everything's all right," he said, but the rangy lineback dun didn't seem to be reassured.

Cody backed out of the stall and had just entered the next one when he heard a clinking sound on the far side of the barn, near the haymow, as if something—or someone—up in the hay had dislodged a small stone or a stick. Cody hadn't wanted to go up in the haymow, not carrying a lantern, but now it looked as if he was going to have to.

But not just yet. He'd wait a minute, just in case it really was Gus up there. The outlaw would've heard the noise, too, and known he'd made a mistake. He'd be alert and ready for Cody.

Cody was going to give him a minute to calm down. He stayed in the stall for a while, patted the horse, and backed out. He was looking toward the haymow, waiting to make his move, when the roof of the barn fell in on him.

When the Ranger woke up, he felt as if his head were wearing a vise—either that or his brain was swelling up so big that it was going to bust right out of his skull.

He doubted the second possibility very much. He wasn't so sure that he even had a brain anymore, not if he was so dumb as to be taken in by the old trick that had fooled him in the barn. Gus had thrown something toward the haymow to get Cody's attention, then sneaked up behind the Ranger and tried to cave in his head.

He'd just about succeeded, too, Cody thought, if the pain was any indication.

Cody opened his eyes. He was back in his room in the Carswell house, and Hope was sitting beside the bed, holding his hand. Hayden Carswell was standing at the foot of the bed, looking at him.

"He's coming to," Carswell said.

Hope tightened her grip on Cody's hand. "Cody," she said, "can you hear me?"

He started to shake his head and was immediately sorry. "I can hear you. But it sounds like you're a long way off."

Hope smiled with relief. "That's only natural. You gave us quite a scare. I wasn't sure how you'd come out of it, to tell the truth. Another blow on the head after the bullet wound might have been enough to kill you."

Cody tried to smile. He wasn't sure whether he was successful. "I told you I had a hard head." He looked at Carswell. "I remember getting hit in the barn. How did I get back here?"

"I found you," Carswell said. "You were lying on the floor and the lantern was beside you. A small blaze had started, but there was no damage. Luckily I got there in time."

"What were you doing there?"

"I asked him to go," Hope said. "You'd been gone for so long that I got worried. So I asked Mr. Carswell to go check on you."

"The first place I went was the barn," Carswell said. "I thought I could see a light shining through the space underneath the door, and so naturally I thought you might be in there with the lantern. You were, but not exactly as I'd expected to find you."

"What about Gus?"

"There was no one else," Carswell said. "I searched the place quickly because I knew that I should get you back to the house as soon as I could, but I was thorough. No one was there but you."

"Gus was there, all right," Cody said, fingering the new lump on his head. "You might've scared him away, but he must've been the one who hit me."

"I'm sure you're right," Carswell agreed. "No doubt he attacked you and then ran away when he heard me coming. There's a back door in the barn."

"Well, he's long gone by now, I reckon," Cody said. "But from what I've seen of the weather tonight, he won't be able to find his way to wherever it is he thought he was going. I expect he'll freeze to death out there on the prairie, and we won't find his bones until springtime. If then."

"What if he didn't try to go anywhere?" Hope said. "What if he's still out there in the barn?"

"He's not in the barn," Carswell said. "I looked through the whole place."

Hope wasn't convinced. "He could've come back."

"I don't think so," Cody said. "Now that he knows we're on to him, he's bound to have cleared out."

"I hope you're right," Carswell said. "I don't want him hanging around here and causing trouble for me and my family."

"If you're worried about him, I'll search the barn again in the morning," Cody said.

"That won't be necessary," Carswell told him. "I'll take care of that myself."

Cody wanted to protest, but his head was throbbing so much that he decided against it. Maybe he'd feel better tomorrow, and if he did, then he could see about looking in the barn. He had to try whatever he could to find Gus. It was hard for him to accept the fact that he'd lost one of his prisoners. Captain Vickery wouldn't be happy about it, and Cody wouldn't blame him. He wasn't happy, either. The only one he had left was Rachel, and she wasn't even the one he'd been sent to bring back.

At the thought of Rachel, Cody had another idea. She had eaten dinner with the family, but then she'd been locked in her room. Cody wondered whether anyone had checked on her.

"I did," Hope said. "Right after you went looking for Gus."

"Did you mention that Gus was missing?"

"No. I didn't know whether you wanted her to know that or not, so I simply didn't say anything. I did look around the room, though, just to see if anyone was hiding there."

Cody wasn't sure how well Hope could have searched the room with Rachel right there and not have given anything away, but he didn't think Gus could've gotten back in the house anyway. And if he had, he couldn't have gotten past the lock on Rachel's door. Unless he had help, of course; there was always that possibility.

"I'd rather no one said anything to her about Gus being gone," Cody said. He was speaking mainly to Carswell, who, he suspected, would be seeing her sooner than any of the others. "I'll have a talk with her in the morning."

"I think you'd better just stay in bed in the morning," Hope told him. "I'm surprised that you feel like talking now."

"I don't," Cody said. "But you don't have to worry about me. I'll be fine in the morning. Just don't say anything to Rachel."

He was looking directly at Carswell as he spoke the last words, but the ranch owner gave no indication that he had anything more than a passing acquaintance with Rachel.

"No one will tell her," Carswell said. "I'll instruct my daughters to say nothing."

Cody thought that the second part might be true, but he really didn't much believe the first. He was sure Carswell would tell Rachel of Gus's disappearance as soon as he saw her, and he would see her as soon as he thought everyone was in bed. It really didn't matter, Cody supposed. He probably couldn't catch Rachel off guard, anyway, and right now the only thing he cared about was sleep.

The next morning, Cody didn't feel as well as he had hoped. Though there was none of the dizziness that had accompanied the bullet wound, he had a sizable headache. He reached up and gingerly touched the knot on his head. It wasn't as big as it had been, but it was still there.

Nevertheless, he got out of bed and cleaned himself up. He had to talk to Rachel.

Hope had the key to Rachel's room, and Cody went to get it from her. She was already dressed and waiting for him, though she told him that she hadn't planned to wake him.

"If you hadn't come, I would've just gone down to breakfast," she said. "I thought you needed to rest. Did you sleep well?"

Cody told her that he had.

"What about visitors?" she teased.

"There weren't any," Cody said. "And I'm just as glad of it. I needed the rest. But now I have to talk to Rachel, on the off chance that she knows something."

"Do you think she'll tell you anything if she does know?"

Cody grinned. "Nope, but I have to ask."

They went to Rachel's room, and though she tried to feign surprise at Gus's escape, Cody was sure that she already knew. The trouble was that he didn't know whether she'd been in touch with Gus or whether Carswell had told her.

"You don't seem very worried about him," Cody said.

Rachel shrugged. "Why should I be? He's been taking care of himself for a long time. He'll get along all right."

"Not in this weather," Cody said.

The day had dawned just as gray and cold as the one before. It was beginning to look as if there wouldn't be a thaw for a good while.

"And what about you?" Hope asked. "Doesn't it bother you that he just went off and left you?"

Rachel gave a bitter laugh. "Why should it? I'd do the same thing if I got the chance."

"But you're not going to get the chance," Cody declared. "I'll see to that."

"Maybe you will," Rachel said. "And maybe you won't."

"What's that supposed to mean?" Cody asked.

"You're the big smart lawman. You figure it out."

"If you're thinking that you can get away," Cody cautioned, "you'd better think twice."

Rachel didn't say a thing. A tiny smile tugged at the corners of her mouth.

"You confessed to a couple of murders to me when we were at Eli's cabin," Cody said, hoping to change the smile to something else. "When we get back to Del Rio, I'm going to see that you face charges for them."

Rachel remained silent. While the smile didn't get any larger, it didn't disappear.

Cody didn't understand why she seemed so confident. Of course, she had a history of getting out of bad situations and making the best of things. Hardly anyone else would've escaped from San Antonio after setting a house on fire and burning up its two occupants, but Rachel had managed to do so. And while her association with Gus might not have been filled with true devotion and romance, the two did seem to have a bond of some kind. Taking everything into account, then, Rachel had been pretty lucky so far, and maybe she was thinking that her luck would continue.

Or maybe she was thinking that someone would intervene on her behalf in one way or another, namely Carswell. Cody didn't know how the rancher would take it if he knew that Rachel would be hauled off to jail for murder. As far as the Ranger knew, no one had told Carswell that part of Rachel's history, and he might've been fooled by her innocent appearance into thinking that she had been misled into a life of outlawry by Gus.

The more Cody thought about it, the more it seemed that he needed to get Rachel away from the Carswell place as soon as possible. The more time she spent with Carswell, the more time he had to become attached to her, and the more time she had to make an escape, either with Carswell's help or without it. And Cody wouldn't put it past Gus to come back for her, if somehow he had managed to make it through the night.

But it was clear that Rachel was going to tell him nothing more, so he and Hope left the room.

"What about Eli?" he asked when they were in the hall. "Could he travel if it clears up tomorrow?"

"I think so," Hope replied. "Let's look in on him."

Reaching Eli's room, they knocked, then entered at his request.

Eli was feeling fine. "I don't hurt much anymore," he told them. "I could ride a horse if I had to."

Cody was still thinking about the wagons. "Maybe you won't have to if Woodley and his flock will go along with us."

"That's a fine idea," Eli said. "You goin' to ask 'em?"

Cody turned toward the door. "As soon as I get the chance."

CHAPTER
11

He got the chance much sooner than he expected. The Reverend Liam Woodley tugged on his sleeve as they were about to enter the dining room. Cody turned and at first didn't see the preacher, who was so short that he barely came up to Cody's shoulder.

"Could I talk to you for a minute, in private?" Woodley asked.

Cody nodded and motioned to Hope and Eli to go on in and eat without him. "Sure. Let's go in the parlor. I've got something that I wanted to ask you, anyway."

Once they were in the parlor, Woodley didn't seem to know how to get started. He talked about the weather and his church and about the revival he'd been going to attend, but he didn't once touch on a subject sensitive enough to require privacy.

Cody tried to put him at his ease. "I know you're anxious to get to Del Rio. I've got a little favor to ask you about that."

Woodley seemed much more comfortable with the idea of granting a favor than with talking about whatever it was that was bothering him. "I'd be pleased to help you out any way I can," he said.

"Well," Cody said, "what I'd like is for you and your flock to go on to Del Rio with me and Dr. Baxter as soon as the weather changes. I don't think that's going to happen today, but by tomorrow we might be able to travel. Eli Peyton and my prisoner will be going along, too. We had a buggy when we started out, but there was an accident on the road, and it's not in any shape to be used. So I'd like to use one of your wagons to haul my prisoner. And I think Eli might be more comfortable riding in a wagon than on a horse."

Woodley heaved a sigh of relief. "That's a favor I'd be delighted to grant. You see, Mr. Cody, I was going to ask you to help us get away from this place."

"Is there something wrong with it?" Cody asked, wondering if the preacher was having the same feelings of unease about the Carswells that he and Hope had.

Woodley lowered his voice until it was hardly more than a whisper. "I think that there is iniquity here, Mr. Cody. Iniquity of the flesh."

Cody frowned. "I'm not sure I follow you."

"Sin, Mr. Cody. I'm talking about carnal sin."

Cody was beginning to catch on. "Did you have a visit in your room last night from one of Carswell's daughters?"

Woodley was deeply shocked. "Of course not! They wouldn't try anything like that with a man of God."

"I'm sorry," Cody said. "I wasn't trying to imply that you'd do anything wrong. But something must've happened to get you upset."

Woodley nodded vigorously. "Indeed it did. I didn't have a visitor, but I have every reason to believe that Deacon Forbes did." He paused and gave Cody a straight look. "And might I ask what made you think of visitors in the first place?"

"I had one myself," Cody told him, understating the number somewhat. "I turned down her offer, though."

"I would certainly hope so, since you're a representative of the law. But I'm afraid that Deacon Forbes yielded to the temptations of the flesh." Woodley shook his head sadly. "And to think that he has a wife and children. I'm sorry that I ever allowed him to come on this trip."

"It's not your fault," Cody told the preacher. "Are you sure about this?"

"As sure as I can be. His room is next to mine, and in the middle of the night I was awakened by someone moaning in the next room. I thought at first that Deacon Forbes might be having some kind of seizure, but before I could get out of bed, I realized that the moans I was hearing weren't *that* kind at all, but were of a far different nature. I was so ashamed that I pulled my pillow over my head, but I could hardly drown them out."

Cody had thought that one or more of the sisters might pay a visit to the other men, so he wasn't exactly shocked. But he was mildly surprised that Forbes had taken advantage of the situation. It seemed to Cody that a man on the way to a religious revival meeting ought to have a little more control over himself.

"So you think it might be a good idea if we moved on?" he said.

"As soon as possible!" Woodley said, looking around the parlor as if he expected one of the women to slip in and assault him right there. "I hate the thought of having to pass another night in this house."

Cody didn't like it any more than Woodley did, for different reasons, but he didn't think there'd be much chance of getting away before night. The weather was so bleak and cold that it looked like the ice would be around for at least another day.

Woodley interrupted his thoughts. "Maybe I ought to speak to Mr. Carswell about the behavior of his children. 'Spare the rod and spoil the child,' as the Good Book says. I think he needs to apply the rod."

Cody wasn't sure the Carswell girls wouldn't in fact enjoy that, but he didn't think it would be appropriate to say so to a preacher. Instead, he said, "We shouldn't tell Carswell what we're thinking about *anything*. Not about his daughters and not about leaving here."

"Why not?" Woodley demanded.

"Because there's a lot that's not right about this place. I don't know just what it is, but there's more going on here than meets the eye. The less these people know about our plans, the better I'll like it."

"But Deacon Forbes—"

"Will just have to deal with his own conscience. Matter of fact, I don't think it'd be a good idea to mention that we're planning on leaving even to him. You never know who he might tell."

"I have a pretty good idea," Woodley said dourly. "Jezebels, the lot of them! The Whore of Babylon!"

The preacher was working up a pretty good head of steam. His seamed face was getting red all the way to the top of his bald head, and his voice was rising.

Cody tried to calm him. "No matter what we think about the women, we'd best keep our plans quiet. I don't want anyone trying to stop us when we leave here. Do you?"

Woodley collected himself. "No, sir, I do not want that. I'll hold my tongue."

"Good. Now, why don't we go in and have breakfast and act like nothing happened."

"I'll try."

Woodley had done a pretty good job, too, Cody thought later, considering that Forbes had been so full of good humor and had cast so many sly looks in the direction of Francesca during breakfast that he had hardly had time to eat. Woodley had watched him with a look of such ill-concealed disgust that Cody had feared for a while that he'd give everything away, but the preacher had refrained from saying anything about his suspicions and finally turned his attention to a conversation between the Evanses and the Prescotts about some upcoming event at the Pandale Baptist Church.

The rest of the day passed slowly and uncomfortably. There was a noticeable tension building up among some of the occupants of the house, and Cody couldn't understand all the reasons for it.

Sure, part of it was due to Woodley's fairly solid suspicions about Forbes's nocturnal activities, and of course Rachel was always a source of anxiety. Gus's escape didn't help matters any, either. There was always the chance that he hadn't died in the cold after all and was lurking around the grounds, waiting for a chance to cause trouble. And then there was Cody's fear that Woodley might inadvertently say something that would give away their plan to leave the next day, but the preacher seemed to be keeping a tight rein on his tongue.

So with all those sources of uneasiness and concern, it was no wonder that there was a bit of apprehension in the air. But there was more to it than that. The vague feeling

of wrongness that Cody had felt on his first day here
had intensified greatly, and he traced it to the behavior
of Carswell and his daughters.

They were still cheerful and talkative, but now and then,
when they thought that no one was observing them, they
would draw aside and whisper urgently to one another.
Carswell himself was often out of sight, and Cody wondered just where the man was spending his time and what
he was up to. There might be a simple explanation, but
Cody didn't know what it was.

Reverend Woodley asked permission to hold another religious service in the afternoon, and Carswell was
pleasant enough about granting it. Cody was afraid that
the message would have to do with sparing the rod, or
maybe with the Whore of Babylon, but Woodley was
circumspect enough to preach briefly on the wanderings
of the tribes of Israel after their flight from Egypt, though
he did come down pretty heavily on the episode with the
golden calf.

All during the service, even the singing, Josiah Forbes
was staring lustfully at Francesca. Cody thought that while
Woodley might not be looking forward to another night in
this house, his deacon surely was.

In fact, Forbes had never looked forward to anything so
much as he looked forward to what he was sure would take
place not long after nightfall. His first visit from Francesca
had been a revelation, and he could hardly keep his eyes
off her all day. The truth of the matter was that Forbes
had once possessed all the qualities Reverend Woodley
thought should be found in the character of a deacon,
but that had been a long time ago, and Forbes's life had
changed a great deal since then.

When he was young man, just married and getting
started in his business, Forbes was a true believer in the
Christian faith, a man who attended church as regularly
as the doors opened, not because he felt it was a duty, but
because it was a pure pleasure to him. He liked to join in
the singing of the hymns, he liked to hear the Scriptures
read, and he took delight in the preaching of the Word.

But as the years went by and Forbes's personal life became increasingly grim, he became less and less a believer and more and more a churchgoer by habit.

He blamed it all on his wife, who wasn't the most passionate of women. She regarded their marital relations as an onerous duty, one that she performed as quickly, cleanly, and efficiently as humanly possible. There was no pleasure for her in it, and therefore none for Forbes.

Even worse, it seemed to him that every time his wife granted him her favors—such as they were—she got pregnant. He had seven children who brought him no more pleasure in the rearing than they had in the creating. The situation hadn't improved with the passing of time, but just as he was in the habit of going to church, he was also in the habit of being a husband and father. He kept on doing it despite the dissatisfaction that his life gave him.

Because he was good at keeping his personal life a secret, most of the community of Pandale had no idea of his feelings about his family. On Sundays he was always at the church with his wife and children, always occupying the same pew. If anyone in town had been asked about him, they'd have responded that he was a religious, responsible family man.

Of course, they knew that he was sour on life. He was never one to keep his opinions to himself, and mostly his opinions were on the pessimistic side. Even Forbes knew that he seldom had a good word to say about anything.

That was why he was on his way to Del Rio. He was well into his middle years, and he'd begun to think heavily on those days in the past when he was a younger and happier man. There had to be some way to recapture those feelings, he had told himself. Maybe one way would be to regain something of the feeling he'd once had when attending church. A renewal was what he needed, a renewal of his old spirit, and when Reverend Woodley had asked if anyone wanted to go to Del Rio to attend a revival service, Forbes had been the first to say he did.

It had seemed like a good idea, a way to get back to something that he'd lost, but when the storm had come along, Forbes had been convinced that they were all going to die out there on the plains, frozen in a freak blizzard.

When Woodley had talked about God working in mysterious ways, Forbes had wanted to kick the preacher's teeth in.

But now Forbes was convinced that God indeed had a purpose in mind for them, or at least for him.

Francesca's visit to his room had proved that. He had been revived in a way that no church meeting could ever have accomplished, and he was sure that he would be equally revived again that night.

Francesca was exciting in ways that he'd never even dreamed of. He had never seen his wife without clothing on, and he had come to hate the sight of her long-sleeved, high-collared white cotton nightgowns, which she would pull up for him—never off—only if all the lights in the house were extinguished. But Francesca had seemed to glory in the sight of her own body. She had undressed slowly and luxuriously in the lamplight, letting Forbes look his fill at her creamy shoulders, her full breasts, her flat stomach, and the red tangle of curls below.

When she came into his bed, she had moved with an urgency of desire that Forbes's wife would never have understood but that was so thrilling to Forbes that he couldn't help crying out in pleasure, even though the Reverend Woodley was in the next room and probably listening. At that point, Forbes hadn't really given a damn. If his wife and children had been in the next room, Forbes wouldn't have been able to restrain the cry.

Forbes didn't know why Francesca had come to him. She hadn't talked much, preferring action to words. But he knew one thing: He wasn't going on to Del Rio with Woodley and the others. Let them go to church; he had other things in mind. Sooner or later he'd have to return to Pandale, to whatever waited for him there, but until he did, he was going to enjoy himself to the fullest.

He knew that some of the others must have suspected what had happened. He could tell that the Ranger was watching him. Well, let him watch. Hell, he could come in the room that night and watch if he wanted to, sell tickets if he had a mind. That wasn't going to stop Forbes. He'd found what he'd been looking for, and he had only one regret: He was sorry that he hadn't found it years before.

• • •

When the long day was finally past and dinner had been served and eaten, Cody stopped by Hope's room. He told her that no matter the weather, they'd be leaving the next day. He also explained that Woodley's group would be coming along with them and told her why.

Hope expressed no shock at Forbes's behavior. "Reverend Woodley has a good heart, and I like the Evanses and the Prescotts, but that man Forbes is not the sort of deacon I've known before. Did you see the way he was looking at Francesca today?"

Cody admitted that he'd noticed. "Not that I blame him," he added.

Hope shook her head and her pale hair danced in the lamplight. "You should be ashamed of yourself, Mr. Cody."

"Yep. Ashamed that I turned her down."

"I don't think you really mean that."

"That's something we'll have to talk over when we get back to town," Cody said.

Hope smiled. "I think so, too." Then she changed the subject. "Does Eli know we'll be leaving?"

"He knows, and Woodley is supposed to tell the Evanses and the Prescotts tonight. But not Forbes. We'll tell him and Rachel at the last minute. You'll need to be ready as early as you can."

"I'll be ready," Hope promised. "I'll be as glad to leave here as anybody."

The next morning Cody was up before daybreak, dressed and on his way to the barn. The air was still cold, but there was a slight breeze from the south, a sure sign of warming, and the sky in the east was lit red by the approach of dawn. Sometime in the night the clouds had rolled away, and Cody was sure that the combination of south wind and sun would melt the ice. Probably most of it would be gone before noon.

He opened the barn door and entered quietly so as not to spook the horses and mules. They stirred sleepily in their stalls, and Cody left the door open so that the light that was gathering in the sky would soon show him the barn's interior. He located the grain supply and fed the animals and then looked around for their harness.

He didn't see the harness in the deep shadows of the barn, but he did see a dark rectangle that he supposed was the door to a tack room. If Carswell kept the harness for his own animals there, he had probably hung the rest in there as well.

Cody pushed the door of the tack room open. The room had a wooden floor, and the door scraped on the wood as it slowly opened. Cody peered inside. The sunlight had reached the barn door by now, but it wasn't yet strong enough to illuminate the tack room. Cody blinked, trying to accustom his eyes to the darkness.

After a few seconds he could make out what seemed to be leather harness on the walls, but there was something else in the room, too, something that made his mouth go dry.

He couldn't be seeing there what he thought he was, he told himself. It just wasn't possible. The darkness and the shadows had to be playing tricks on him.

Feeling his stomach lurch, he went back to the barn door and opened it wider. Then he returned to the tack room and pushed that door farther open as well.

What he saw caused hot bile to rise and burn in his throat. He swallowed it back down and forced himself to step into the room for a closer look.

Gus Peyton hadn't left the ranch after all, but he certainly was never going to give anyone trouble again. And Cody didn't think that he'd gotten where he was because he wanted to be there. He'd had help.

Nobody would choose to end up as Gus had.

Centered overhead, a wooden beam ran down the length of the room. Hanging from the beam was Gus's nude, frozen corpse, head down, his lank hair only inches above the floor. And spaced at regular intervals along the beam, other bodies were hanging.

Cody couldn't make out their features well in the dim light. Fighting back his revulsion, he forced himself to go closer to look at their faces. He'd seen dead men before, and plenty of them, but he'd never seen anything like this. He had to swallow hard again.

He was pretty certain that he knew who three of the men were—Pete, Swain, and Ernie. Plainly the Carswells had made a trip back to where the three outlaws had been killed and brought them to the barn, though Cody didn't know when they could have done so.

There were two other men hanging there also, but Cody didn't recognize either of them. He wondered where they'd come from and whether the Carswells had found their bodies or had murdered them. Because it was clear that the Carswells knew what they were doing. The tack room had been altered for use as a slaughterhouse.

All the men's throats had been cut, and the blood had drained out of them into a channel cut in the floor of the room. Worse, they had been gutted like deer. They hung there now like so many slabs of beef waiting for a butcher to cut them up into steaks and roasts.

A horrible thought occurred to Cody. His stomach roiled, and again he fought back the urge to vomit. He willed the thought out of his mind, but he knew that what was happening at the Carswell ranch was something a lot worse than he ever would've imagined. He'd have to arrest Carswell and his daughters and get them to Del Rio somehow.

It was no wonder that he and Hope had experienced some sort of foreboding about this place. It was a butcher shop, and the animals being butchered were human beings.

Still feeling sick, Cody left the tack room and closed the door behind him. He walked across the barn, his legs wobbly. He felt almost as if he'd been shot in the head again.

When he reached the door, he started outside, but suddenly a hand came down on his shoulder, reaching out of the dark shadows near the door to grab his coat and toss him back into the barn with inhuman strength. He went sprawling on the hay-littered ground, landing hard on his side.

Cody rolled over and scrambled to his feet. The immediacy of the attack took his mind off the sight in the tack room, and he concentrated on defending himself from his assailant, who now pulled the barn door shut and advanced on the Ranger.

The man was considerably bigger than Cody, with wide shoulders and powerful arms. Cody couldn't see his face well in the dim light that remained in the barn, but he could tell that the man was big enough to carry a corpse with ease.

Cody reached for his pistol, but the man was on him in a flash, knocking the gun from his hand and flinging him halfway across the barn. The Ranger's head, already abused well beyond its normal limits, rang like a bell, and he shook it in hopes of clearing away the noise. But he should have paid more attention to his attacker, because before his head was clear, the man had crossed the space between them, swinging his big fists like hammers.

Cody ducked under one blow and threw a hard right into the man's bearded face, cracking his nose and causing blood to spurt out of it.

The man howled and backed up, and Cody pursued his advantage. He and his attacker traded blows until the man managed to elude one of the Ranger's punches and grabbed the Ranger in a bear hug, lifting him six inches from the floor. Cody could smell the man's rank odor, a combination of sweat and fear.

The man was extremely powerful, and his thick arms began to squeeze the breath from Cody's body. Cody rained blows on the man's head, but he simply grunted and kept on squeezing.

Cody figured that there were two possibilities. Either the man was going to break all his ribs or he was going to suffocate him. Neither alternative appealed to the Ranger, so he stopped his struggling and went limp in his adversary's arms.

The sudden lack of resistance created a second of hesitation in the man's mind and a momentary easing of the pressure on Cody's ribs. The Ranger acted. Grabbing the man's shoulders, he hooked his heels behind the man's calves and jerked his legs out from under him. The man fell backward with Cody on top.

But Cody's advantage lasted only a fraction of a second. Almost before the Ranger knew what was happening, the immensely strong man had flipped him over and straddled his chest.

A fist that seemed to be the size of a saddle slammed Cody's head against the floor, sending a jolt of pain from his crown to his toes. One more blow like that, on top of all the other jolts his poor head had gotten lately, Cody thought, and he'd be addled for life. His fingers scrabbled at the floor as he searched for something—anything!—that would help him. They touched the butt of his pistol. He grabbed it and swung it up from the floor in a smooth arc, clouting the man in the side of the head just before his fist connected with Cody's jaw a second time. The man slumped to the side but didn't go down. It would take more than one whack to put him out.

So Cody gave him another one.

The man slid off Cody and half lay, half sat beside him, shaking his head and breathing hard.

Cody hit him again.

This time he went down and stayed down.

CHAPTER
12

Something was wrong. Hope Baxter was sure of it. Just what was wrong she couldn't have said, except that it was now fully daylight and Cody hadn't yet come for her. The weather was going to be all right for traveling, and they should have been well on their way by now. She was beginning to get very worried that something had happened to the Ranger.

She looked out the window, past the water dripping off the roof of the house from the ice already beginning to melt, but the barn wasn't visible from the side of the house her room was on. Hope wondered if someone had seen Cody and tried to stop him from leaving. She still wasn't sure why they had to worry about that. After all, Cody was a Ranger. Hope didn't think that Carswell would try to prevent him from performing his duty, no matter how fond the rancher had become of Rachel.

A knock sounded on the door, and Hope started. Then she hurried over to open it.

"It's about time you—" The rest of the sentence never got spoken. It wasn't Cody at her door; it was Francesca Carswell. And her sisters were knocking on the other doors, rousing everyone. "What's happening?" Hope asked. "Isn't it a little early for breakfast?"

"Breakfast?" Francesca said. "Did anybody say anything about breakfast? We're here to get everyone together in the parlor. We're having a meeting."

"A meeting? You mean that Reverend Woodley—"

Francesca laughed. It wasn't a pleasant sound. "To hell with the preacher. This is going to be a different kind of meeting. I think it's going to be a lot more interesting to you than the ones that old jackass has been having."

Hope didn't like the way Francesca was talking. She had formerly spoken in a somewhat refined manner that belied her actions in visiting the rooms of two different men, but now she was showing a crudity of speech that matched her behavior.

Despite her misgivings, Hope went down to the parlor with the others. She wanted to know what was going on, but she didn't mention Cody. She wondered if the sisters were aware that he wasn't among the group. If they were, they didn't remark on the fact.

When everyone was gathered in the parlor, a buzz of conversation filled the room as they all talked at once, trying to determine if anyone knew what was going on. Apparently only the sisters did, and they weren't saying.

"Where's Mr. Carswell?" Hope asked finally, noticing that the rancher was also missing from the room.

"That's a good question," Francesca said. "Maybe he's with your Mr. Cody."

"He's not my Mr. Cody," Hope replied, blushing. "And I don't know where he is."

"Someone does," Francesca said, looking at Woodley.

"I assure you that I don't," the preacher told her.

"I thought it was a sin for a preacher to lie," Brenna said, laughing nastily.

Woodley was offended by her implication. While he might have an idea where Cody was, he certainly didn't know for sure.

He told Brenna, "I'll have you know that I am not a liar. Where Mr. Cody goes is his own business, not mine."

"Maybe that's right," Phoebe said. "And maybe it's not. Maybe where he goes is everybody's business."

Josiah Forbes, who was standing near Francesca and looking at her with longing, smiled and said, "I don't know why you're being so mysterious about this. Why don't you just tell us why you wanted us all to meet?"

"We will," said Francesca. "As soon as Father gets here."

"And when will that be?" Hope asked.

"It won't be long," Francesca said. "While we're waiting, just sit down and relax. Make yourselves at home."

"That's right," Diana said. "We're very hospitable. Our house is your house."

At that all the sisters laughed, and Hope felt as if one of the now-melting icicles had been slipped down the back of her dress. She wished Cody were there; she was sure that if he was, he could make things right.

Cody rolled the big unconscious man over and studied his face. He was heavily bearded, but Cody thought he saw a vague resemblance to Francesca. Could this man be a relative? A Carswell son, perhaps? He hadn't been in evidence around the house, and Carswell had never mentioned him, but that didn't mean anything. Carswell hadn't mentioned the tack room, either.

It suddenly struck Cody that he shouldn't have been able to see the man's face so clearly; there was much more light in the barn than there should have been with the door closed.

Cody turned to find that the door had been opened and sunlight was streaming in. Standing just inside the doorway and casting a long shadow across the straw-strewn floor was Hayden Carswell. He was cradling a double-barreled shotgun in his hands. The gun was held casually, but it was pointed in Cody's general direction.

Cody stood up and said, "I wish you'd gotten here a little sooner. I could've used a little help."

"I'm sure you could have," Carswell said. "But the truth of the matter is, you shouldn't have come out here to the barn alone, Mr. Cody." He looked at the man Cody had knocked out, who still lay motionless. "I hope you haven't hurt Luther too badly. He's my only son, you see, and I'm afraid that I'd be very upset with you if he were severely injured."

"I think he'll be all right," Cody said, equally diffident. "He was trying to do more damage to my head than I did to his."

Carswell raised the shotgun so that the barrels were pointing directly at Cody's midsection. "I hope you're right. But be that as it may, I think that you should drop your pistol and your knife, Mr. Cody."

Cody hesitated. He didn't want to let go of his gun.

"Now, Mr. Cody," Carswell said, pulling back the shotgun's two hammers one at a time with his thumb. "Drop them now. Surely you don't want to go up against this scattergun with a pistol. You might get off a shot, but unless you kill me instantly, you'll be blown apart."

Carswell had a point. Cody put the pistol on the floor, followed by the big bowie knife.

Carswell nodded his approval. "Very good. Now, shall we go back to the house? I believe there's a meeting being held, and we don't want to be the only ones left out."

Cody glanced at Luther. "What about him?"

"We'll leave him here for the time being. He's used to being left just a bit outside the family circle. Now, come along." Carswell gestured toward the door with the shotgun. "You can walk in front."

Following Carswell's orders, Cody led the way back to the house. When they had entered the front door, Carswell said, "Go to the parlor."

Cody obeyed the instructions reluctantly. He had no idea what would happen next, but he didn't intend to wind up like Gus Peyton.

Reaching the double-doored entrance to the parlor, Cody saw that the others had all gathered there. He thought about trying to give them some kind of warning, but Carswell prodded him in the back with the shotgun's cold steel barrels.

"I'll do the talking for right now, Mr. Cody," Carswell said as they stepped into the room. Standing immediately behind the Ranger, he signaled his daughters. "Francesca, you and Brenna go to the barn and see about your brother. He's had a rather difficult time with Mr. Cody."

Francesca and Brenna nodded and left the room hurriedly.

Forbes got up and started after them. "I'll help Francesca," he said.

"That won't be necessary," Carswell told him, shifting slightly to the right and allowing all of them to see the shotgun for the first time.

"Cody," Hope said raggedly, "what's going on?"

"You'll have to ask Carswell about that," Cody answered. "He's the one with the gun."

"But not the only one," Diana said, and she and Phoebe produced guns of their own, small-caliber revolvers that they handled with complete confidence and familiarity.

"What is this?" Forbes blustered. "Why have you suddenly turned against us? And who's this brother you're talking about?"

Cody could see that none of the "guests" understood what was happening, but he knew well enough. They weren't guests at all, and they never had been. Cody had thought that Rachel and Gus were the only two prisoners here, but so were he and all these other people who'd had the misfortune to come to the Carswell house. As he thought about Gus, he wondered if they'd all receive the same sentence that had been meted out to the outlaw.

"The 'brother' is my son, Luther," Carswell said, answering Forbes's question. "I don't believe that you've met him."

"They can meet him now," Francesca said. She and Brenna stood at the parlor entrance, flanking a darkly glowering Luther, who looked at Cody with undisguised hatred.

Cody was sure now that Luther was the one who had jumped him in the barn while he was looking for Gus. No one had wanted Cody to stumble on the tack room, and Luther was the one appointed to stand guard. He just hadn't gotten up early enough today. The existence of the burly Luther also explained how the bodies of Pete, Swain, and Ernie had been fetched. The Ranger hadn't been able to figure out when the other Carswells could have done it, but it would've been easy enough for Luther. And he supposed that Luther was the one who'd killed Gus.

Thinking of Gus reminded Cody of someone else, and he wondered if Rachel had met Gus's fate.

"Is Rachel here?" he said, looking around the parlor. "I don't see her."

"She's still in her room," Francesca said. "I forgot about her."

"Go fetch her now," Carswell ordered. "Do you have your key?"

"Yes," Francesca said, reaching in a pocket and bringing it out. She held it up for her father to see, then left to get Rachel. Forbes again watched her go, but this time his expression was more one of puzzlement than of longing.

The family having extra keys explained how they had spirited Gus out of the locked room to kill him, Cody thought.

"What do you plan to do with us?" Reverend Woodley asked. "You still haven't answered that question."

"We'll wait for Rachel," Carswell replied. "She should hear the answers to these questions, too."

Cody noted a distinct sense of familiarity in Carswell's voice. He was clearly on an intimate basis with her, just as Hope had speculated.

Francesca brought Rachel into the room a few minutes later, and Cody decided to try driving a wedge between Carswell and Gus's alleged wife. "Was it you who murdered Gus and strung him up in the barn?" he demanded of Carswell.

There was shock on the faces of everyone but the Carswells at Cody's question.

"Gus is dead?" Eli said.

"That's right," Cody said. He faced Rachel. "Your husband."

Carswell didn't appear concerned by Cody's remarks. "You're a clever man, Cody, but Rachel's loyalty has already been transferred to someone else. Isn't that right, my dear?"

Rachel smiled at him. "If you say so."

"And besides," Carswell said, "I don't think that any of these others really care who killed Gus Peyton. He was an outlaw and a killer, a prisoner of the law. Why should they feel sympathy for him?"

"He was my brother," Eli said hoarsely. "I'm the one who turned him in to the law. I didn't think he'd be killed by somebody worse'n he was."

Carswell shrugged. "These things happen. But the truth is, I didn't kill Gus." He paused and looked proudly at his daughters. "Brenna did."

There were gasps from Sue Beth Prescott and Nancy Evans at that bit of news, and Eli's mouth fell open. But Rachel seemed unconcerned.

"She's quite a capable young woman," Carswell said. "She had some help from Luther, who did the heavy work of carrying Gus to the barn, but Brenna is particularly good with a knife, and though Mr. Cody is the only one of you who's seen her handiwork, I think he'll vouch for what I've said. That's not to say that my other daughters aren't equally skillful, and Luther is quite a hand with a blade as well. Isn't that right, son?"

Luther nodded, smiling at his father's praise.

Cody knew that what they were hearing was as good as a death sentence. Carswell wouldn't be speaking so freely to a group of people that he expected to leave his property alive.

But Cody wasn't the sort to give up, and he figured that as long as Carswell was talking, it might be a good idea to find out as much as he could about what was going on at the ranch house.

"I'm glad you've got such a talented family," he said. "But I don't see what good that kind of talent can do a person."

Carswell thought for a minute. Then he said, "There's no need for pretense any longer, I suppose. I'm sure you've figured most of it out for yourself, but the fact is that since my family's talents don't exactly lend themselves to legitimate pursuits, we make our living in a slightly unusual way."

"You kill people?" Forbes said in a choked voice. "You make a living by killing people?"

"That's more or less correct," Carswell said. "As you might recall, Mr. Cody, I told you that we had moved around a great deal. A business like ours isn't appreciated just anywhere."

"You call it a business?" Woodley thundered. "I call it *evil*! 'Thou shalt not kill,' sayeth the Lord! 'Thou shalt not—' "

"Thou shalt shut thy mouth," Carswell said, "or I'll have Brenna take you outside and slit your gizzard.

Then we'll see what you have to say about abominations."

Brenna laughed. "I'd like doing that, you know."

Everyone could tell that she meant it.

"You see?" Carswell said. "Talent *and* desire. An unbeatable combination. But back to your question, Mr. Forbes, we do make a good living. We rob the people we kill, mostly unwary travelers who happen by on their way to somewhere else . . . somewhere they never arrive. If anyone should come looking for them, which is highly unlikely, we simply say that we never saw them."

"But that's . . . that's . . ." Forbes's voice trailed off. He didn't know what to say.

Woodley did. "Abominable! An abomination in the sight of the Lord!"

"You can put it that way if you want to, Preacher, but you'll remember that I've asked you to be quiet. Brenna would like nothing more than to silence you with a knife blade across your throat."

Woodley bridled at the threat but recognized the seriousness of it. He closed his mouth.

"That's better," Carswell said. "And Mr. Forbes, you should know as well as anyone that we don't merely take and give nothing in return. We give as good as we get. Most of you here have been offered a sampling of the pleasures to be found here, have you not?"

No one said anything, but Cody thought that most of them knew what he meant.

"It's not our fault that some of you failed to take advantage of the opportunity," Carswell went on, looking at Hope. "Not that all of you turned it down. Isn't that right, Mr. Forbes?"

Forbes looked at the floor and said nothing.

"I think we can all see that Mr. Forbes knows what I mean," Carswell said. "I'm sorry my daughters didn't get around to you, Mr. Peyton," he said to Eli. "But don't take it personally. I assure you they would have—had Mr. Cody's inquisitiveness not ruined everything. By the way, we didn't offer anything to the Evanses and the Prescotts, since they are, after all, married. I respect marriage as much as the next man."

What a hypocrite, Cody thought, glancing at Rachel, who seemed to find nothing unusual in Carswell's statement. In fact, she seemed to be looking at him with admiration.

"Now, of course, Luther is a problem," Carswell said. "We have to keep him out of sight of our visitors because Luther doesn't look nearly so attractive as the girls, not even to women, though it's no fault of his own, I suppose."

"I don't know about that," Cody put in. "He could use a bath. That might help."

Luther growled low in his throat, and his fingers curled and uncurled at his sides as if demonstrating what he would have liked to do with them around Cody's neck.

"I wouldn't push Luther too far, Mr. Cody," Carswell warned. "He doesn't like you very much, and while he generally does what I say, I can't always keep him under control. That's why he has his own part of the house to himself. To remove him from the way of temptation."

"The third floor," Cody guessed.

Carswell nodded. "Correct. We keep him up there out of sight so that he doesn't frighten anyone or harm them before I give the word. All of you are being granted a rare privilege. Most people never get to meet Luther. Not until their time has come, that is."

"And now that we've seen him, what does that mean?" Cody asked.

"Ah, yes, that is the question," Carswell said with a smile. "I'll have to think about that. It's really too bad that you had to go to the barn alone, as I said."

"You were going to kill us anyway, weren't you?"

"Sooner or later, yes, of course. But now it appears that it might have to be sooner."

"I don't know why you didn't just do it to begin with," Cody said. "Eli and I were half dead already. It would've been easy for you."

"We didn't kill you then for the same reason that Luther didn't kill you the first time you visited the barn," Carswell said. "We found you interesting."

"Interesting?" Hope repeated. She had worked her way slowly to Cody's side. "What do you mean by that?"

Carswell deferred the answer to one of his daughters. "You explain it, Phoebe."

Phoebe was happy to do so. "It's not easy being all alone out here. We hardly ever get to go anywhere, and nobody ever comes to visit us." She smiled, displaying dimples. "At least, no one ever comes on purpose. So we have to take advantage of the company when we can."

"She's not doing a very good job of explaining," Francesca said impatiently. "What she means is that things can get pretty boring for four sisters and a brother when you don't have anybody around but your family. We all like each other, but everybody needs a little entertainment now and then."

"So you're the entertainment," Phoebe finished. "You and whoever else comes by."

Francesca looked at Forbes. "But like our father said, we give as good as we get. Weren't you entertained, Mr. Forbes?"

Forbes looked as if he wanted to speak but the words stuck in his throat.

"And what happens when the entertainment is over?" Cody asked. "I guess Gus found out the answer to that one."

"He sure did," Brenna said. "We thought it'd be fun to let him think he was going to escape. That added amusement to it, him thinking that I was going to help him get away." She smiled brightly. "And I did, in a way. Didn't I?"

"Of course you did," Carswell said. "He escaped his captors, just as you promised."

"But then the entertainment was over," Cody said.

"You might say that," Carswell admitted. "But you're leaving out the most exciting part of all."

"What's that?" Cody asked.

"The killing itself," Carswell leered. "Isn't that right, children?"

"Oh, yes," Diana said, a rapturous smile lighting her face. "There's really nothing like it. It's better than anything."

Her sisters' eyes glowed. It was plain that they agreed with her.

"It's even better than what we did in bed," Francesca said, looking at Forbes. "A lot better."

"Indeed it is," Carswell agreed, a faraway look in his eyes. "It's by far the biggest thrill of all."

Even Luther smiled. "Yeah," he said. "Yeah."

Cody realized it was the first time he'd heard Luther utter a word.

He also realized something else: Carswell and his entire family were more than just killers. They were all insane.

CHAPTER
||||||||||||||||||||||||| **13** |||||||||||||||||||||||||

The thought of Hayden Carswell's sanity, or lack of it, didn't enter Rachel's mind. She received an almost sexual thrill at his words.

She had only contempt for the others, because it was clear that they didn't understand what Carswell was talking about. For her his words were like a revelation. She had never thought she'd meet anyone who'd express feelings about killing that matched her own.

Even Gus, though he was a hardened criminal, killed only out of necessity, not passion. He hadn't known a thing about the pure thrill of excitement that came when you knew you were the direct cause of another person's death, that you and you alone had taken from someone the most precious possession that they had—life itself.

Gus took money because he needed it, and he killed to get it. But it was the money that mattered to him, not the killing. Rachel understood that, which was why she'd never told even Gus the whole story about the deaths of her uncle and aunt. They had died in the house that Rachel set afire, that much was true. But there was more to the story than that. While her aunt and uncle were out of the house earlier that day, Rachel had jammed shut their bedroom windows, ensuring that they wouldn't open; and after she had set their room afire—by tiptoeing in while the couple was asleep and liberally sprinkling kerosene around, then igniting it—she had jammed the bedroom door as well. As the blaze consumed her aunt and uncle, Rachel hid outside in the shadows and listened to their dying screams—the most thrilling sounds she had ever heard.

Even Gus, as cold-hearted as he was, wouldn't have understood that, but Hayden Carswell would. Rachel knew that this was the man for her, and she planned on telling him so the first chance she got.

Josiah Forbes looked at Francesca Carswell with sick eyes. He could hardly believe what he'd heard in the last few minutes, but he knew that it must be true, as horrible as it seemed.

The really terrible thing to Forbes, however, wasn't what he'd learned about Francesca, but what he'd learned about himself. He knew that his desire to hold Francesca in his arms again—to feel her naked flesh, to feast his eyes on her ripe, naked body—had in no way decreased.

He was, if anything, even more excited about her than before, and he was disgusted with himself for feeling that way. He was a deacon in the church, a respected businessman in his small community, a married man with a family—and still he felt a hard tingle of desire for a woman he now knew to be a participant in murder.

He knew what the Reverend Woodley, the Evanses, and the Prescotts would think of him for feeling what he did, but he found that he couldn't help himself. He never wanted to see his family again. He didn't give a damn about his business. And he didn't care if he never again set foot inside a church. All he cared about was Francesca, and if that meant he had to become what she was, he could do that, too.

Or he thought he could. All he asked was the chance. He would wait and watch, and when the chance came, he would take advantage of it.

He prayed that the chance would come soon.

Cody was more worried now than he had been before Carswell's statement. If Carswell had been a rational man, Cody could at least have discussed matters with him in a logical, reasonable way. Now it appeared that logic and reason were not a part of Carswell's makeup.

He thought of all the bodies in the barn. Why were they there? Why hadn't they been buried? Cody remembered the first appalling thought that had occurred to him, and he was filled with revulsion as he realized that the thought might actually have a basis in fact. He felt that he had to know.

"Aside from the thrill," he said, "there's still something I don't quite understand."

"What's that?" Carswell asked.

"Why are there so many bodies in the barn?"

"So many?" Hope said, unable to conceal the small tremor of surprise and fear in her voice. "You mean that Gus isn't the only one?"

"That's what I mean, all right," Cody told her. "Gus's partners are there, all three of them. And two more that I didn't recognize." He addressed Carswell again. "Why didn't you just bury them? I can understand about Gus. The ice storm's probably made digging impossible. But why are the others in there? And why go after those three that Eli and I killed? Why not just bury them where they died after you robbed their bodies?"

Carswell smirked. "I think that you have certain suspicions about why the bodies are there, Mr. Cody," he said. "You saw them, after all."

Cody had grown up on the Texas frontier. He had seen all manner of examples of man's inhumanity—women who had been raped, men who had been scalped—but what Carswell was implying went far beyond anything Cody had ever experienced.

"You're telling me that you use them for . . ." Cody's voice trailed off. He couldn't make himself complete the sentence.

Carswell didn't have any qualms about it, however. "Food, yes. We use them for food. The corpses keep very well in this cold weather, Mr. Cody, especially if they're drained of blood and disemboweled. You never know when you might run short of provisions in a bad winter like the one we're having this year."

"Sweet Jesus," Kenneth Prescott said hoarsely, his voice full of fear and disgust. "Sweet loving Jesus."

His wife and Nancy Evans wrapped their arms around one another and started sobbing uncontrollably.

"You don't mean that," William Evans said to Carswell, his voice firm. "You're just tryin' to scare us."

He and Prescott tried to comfort their wives, but without much success. The women's sobs just got louder as their husbands whispered soothing words in their ears.

The thought that Cody had earlier banished from his mind returned, and he found himself thinking back over the meals he'd eaten the past few days. But he couldn't remember anything that had tasted unfamiliar, and he couldn't remember seeing any hunks cut from the bodies in the barn, which was much more literally a butcher shop than he'd thought.

"I assure you that I'm not trying to frighten you," Carswell said. "Everything I've said is true. Isn't it, Luther?"

Luther smiled and nodded. "Yeah," he said. "Yeah."

Somehow Luther's simple smile was as chilling as his father's explanation—and the white, even teeth of the smiling, nodding sisters were even more frightening.

Cody looked at Josiah Forbes, who seemed to be a mass of quivering fear. Large round tears rolled down the man's cheeks, and his whole body was shaking in his clothes. Nevertheless, he was still looking at Francesca with something like desire.

Reverend Woodley touched Cody's arm. "I demand that you arrest these people immediately. They're even worse than I thought. Abomination isn't a strong enough word. I don't know a word strong enough to say what they are, but I do know that they'll be destroyed by God if man can't do the job. They'll be like Ahab, and the dogs will lick their blood."

"It won't be my blood that's being licked," Carswell said. "And it won't be dogs that do the licking." He ran a red tongue suggestively around his lips. "Do you take my meaning?"

Woodley stood his ground, glaring at Carswell without fear. He looked to Cody like a small, weathered tree that had survived hard, dry summers and long, cold winters. The Ranger figured that Woodley was someone he could rely on if there came a chance for escape.

And so was Eli. The rancher was naturally frightened, but he was relatively calm. There was wariness but nothing of fear in his eyes as he watched Carswell and the rest of his family. Hope, too, was less disturbed by Carswell's sickening confessions than Cody would've thought. He smiled inwardly. He should've known better than to judge her. She'd fooled him before, and no doubt her medical training had exposed her to all manner of mutilations and amputations. He should have guessed that a little cannibalism wouldn't turn a single blond hair on her head.

And in spite of their wives' near hysteria, Evans and Prescott seemed to Cody to be bearing up pretty well, so that meant Cody had plenty of people he could rely on if he could just come up with a plan. He'd been in some tight spots before now and gotten out of them. He'd never been in a situation quite as weird as this one, but while things didn't look good, he wasn't about to give up looking for a way out of the deadly mess he was in.

He told himself that there was always a way out if you were still alive, which was a consoling thought.

It would've been even more of a consolation if he believed it.

Rachel, on the other hand, knew exactly what her way out was going to be.

Hayden Carswell was going to be her new husband. She was going to be a part of the family.

"Hayden," she said, "do you remember what you were saying about giving as good as you got?"

Carswell smiled at her. "Of course, my dear. And I do hope you enjoyed what you got."

"Oh, yes," Rachel said. "I sure did. But what I was going to ask you was, how did you like what you got?"

Carswell looked thoughtful. Finally he said, "Very much. But of course I can't let something like that affect my judgment."

"I wouldn't want you to do that," Rachel said. "But I wanted you to know that what you got was just a small sample of what I can give you."

"That's very generous of you," Carswell said. "But now that you know about us, you might not care to carry on with our relationship."

Rachel looked at him quizzically. "Why not? You liked

it; I liked it. I can't think of a single reason to stop. In fact, I'd like to make our union a permanent thing."

"Don't listen to her, Father," Francesca snapped. "You know that we've never allowed anyone who's not a member of the family to join us."

"Yeah," Luther said, rubbing his hand on his head where Cody had hit him. "Yeah."

Francesca went on, "We all know that she's hardly the first woman you've ever slept with, and of course she won't be the last. We can't break our rules for her."

"Of course Rachel won't be the last woman I sleep with," Carswell said. He looked at Hope. "In fact, I might be able to persuade one in particular to share my bed, now that she knows she might be able to prolong her life by doing so."

"I'd rather share my bed with a rattlesnake," Hope said scornfully. "You can't persuade me to do anything."

"You see?" Rachel said. "She doesn't understand you. Nobody here understands you but me. I know exactly what you were talking about when you said how killing was the biggest thrill of all." She looked around at the others. "You could see how they felt about that. They think you're disgusting. But I don't. I feel the same way you do. Just thinking about it gets me aroused."

A little shiver went over her body, and Carswell eyed her with interest.

"She's lying," Francesca said, tossing her long red hair. "Can't you see what she's doing? She's just trying to save her own life. Remember, we killed her husband. Even if you break the rules and let her join us, you're never going to be able to trust her."

"That's a good point," Carswell said. "What do you have to say to that, Rachel?"

"You can trust me," Rachel said with a guileless look that made her appear to be about fifteen years old. "Just give me a chance to prove it."

"And just how would you go about proving anything?" Francesca asked.

Carswell's face lit up. "I think I have an answer to that. Would you be willing to kill someone if I asked you to, Rachel?"

"Sure," Rachel said eagerly. "I'd like that. Who?"

"That would be up to you," Carswell said. "Give her your pistol, Francesca."

Francesca didn't want to obey. "What if she shoots *me*?"

"Then you'll have the satisfaction of knowing that after you're dead, I'll shoot her in the belly with this shotgun. But I don't think she'd risk shooting a member of the family she wants to join. Would you, Rachel?"

"Nope. But I still don't know who you *do* want me to kill."

Carswell waved a hand. "Look around you. The room is full of possibilities. You can take your pick. Give her the pistol, Francesca."

Francesca handed it over reluctantly. "Even if she does kill somebody, it's still against the rules to let anyone join the family."

"I make the rules," Carswell said. "And I can change them. Well, Rachel?"

Rachel looked at the .32 pistol Francesca had given her, smiling as she balanced it in her hand. Without warning she turned and shot Josiah Forbes in the middle of the forehead.

The gunshot echoed like thunder in the room.

In the stunned silence that followed, Deacon Josiah Forbes, a look of terrible surprise on his face, toppled forward and crashed to the floor. He was dead before he could even cry out. A pool of dark red blood formed under his head and seeped into the throw rug nearby.

Sue Beth Prescott and Nancy Evans began screaming and weeping louder than ever.

Cody was practically in a daze. He had never thought that Rachel would act so quickly. He hadn't even had a chance to try to stop her.

"Gentlemen," Carswell said to Prescott and Evans, "please control your wives. I would hate to have to silence them in the way that Mr. Forbes has been silenced."

The men whispered urgently to the sobbing women, who gradually calmed themselves, though their shoulders continued to shake in silence.

Rachel handed the pistol back to Francesca. "Thanks. I appreciate the loan."

Carswell beamed at her with approval. "You've certainly demonstrated that you don't mind a little bloodletting."

"Like I told you, I enjoyed it. You want me to do it again?"

Carswell shook his head. "Once is sufficient, though I have to admit that I'm puzzled about one thing. Why kill Mr. Forbes? Why not Mr. Cody or your brother-in-law? After all, they're the ones responsible for your husband's capture, and he wouldn't be dead if they had left him alone. And they're responsible for your own capture besides."

"Hell, I thought about that, but I decided that a quick bullet in the head was too good for them. I'd like it a lot better if I could see them die real slow. They ought to suffer, too, like Gus did with that bullet wound, not get out quick and clean like Forbes. Anyway, he talked too much."

Carswell laughed. "You have a point. Several points, in fact. Maybe you can become one of us, after all."

"Yeah," Luther said. "Yeah."

Cody could tell from Francesca's expression that the eldest daughter didn't agree and neither did her sisters, but they kept their mouths shut. All of them except Francesca seemed a bit afraid of Carswell. Cody didn't blame them.

Carswell gave his son a fatherly pat on the back. "I'm glad to see that you agree with me, Luther. Why don't you take Mr. Forbes's body away now? Put it in the tack room with the others. Phoebe, you go with him and help him prepare it."

Luther grabbed Forbes's corpse under the armpits and heaved it up. The toes of the deacon's boots dragged across the floor as Luther pulled the body out of the room. Forbes's bloody forehead rubbed against the front of Luther's coat, but Luther either didn't notice or didn't care.

Phoebe held the front door open, and then Cody heard it close behind them.

"We'll have to lock the rest of you up, of course,"

Carswell said when the body was cleared away. "But Rachel can remain free for the time being."

"You won't be sorry," Rachel assured him, sidling up to him. "You're gonna like having me around."

"That remains to be seen," Carswell said.

Cody thought that the patriarch might not be entirely convinced of Rachel's suitability as a family member, but the Ranger didn't know why. It seemed to him that she'd fit right in.

Carswell turned to his daughters. "Search everyone and make sure that they don't have any weapons concealed on them. And take any valuables that you find. We might as well be paid a bit for our trouble."

The sisters did their work swiftly. Reverend Woodley didn't carry a weapon, but they relieved him of an ornate pocket watch. Prescott and Evans gave up their pistols, as did Eli. The women gave up their rings and pins.

"Now," Carswell said, "there's the little matter of where we're going to put you."

Rachel had a suggestion. "Why not kill them right now? All except Eli and the Ranger. I'd like to think of something special for those two."

"Don't be in such a rush," Carswell said. "If you're going to be a member of our family, Rachel, you're going to have to learn how things are done. Remember what Francesca and Phoebe said about entertainment? And remember what I said about giving as good as we get? We still operate that way, even if our guests know what fate is waiting for them later."

"That's all right by me," Rachel said. "But what's the entertainment? Seems to me like all the fun's gone out of things now if you're just gonna lock them up."

"There will be more entertainment to come later on," Carswell said. "First we have to take care of them for the rest of the day. What do you think, Francesca?"

"We'll have to watch them," Francesca replied. "I don't trust that Ranger, or any of the rest of them, either."

Carswell agreed. "A sound suggestion, so let's not lock them in separate rooms. That would make them too hard to watch. We'll use two rooms, one for the married couples and one for the rest. As I said, I respect the institution of marriage, and I'm sure that the husbands and wives will have some things to say to one another on their last day together."

"And then what?" Rachel asked.

"And then we'll all come together in the evening for a final meal." Carswell looked at Woodley. "A sort of 'last supper,' you might say."

He smiled wolfishly. He didn't have to say anything else. Everyone knew exactly what he meant.

CHAPTER
14

Cody stood looking out the bedroom window. The sun was shining brightly, and the world was wet with melting ice. It was going to be mighty muddy before long, but it still would've been a good day to travel. Even slogging through mud would've been better than having to stay locked up in one small room waiting for night to come, knowing what Carswell had in mind for them after supper.

Diana had been left on guard in the hallway, but Cody had thought at first they might have a chance for escape by going through the window. There was no possibility of that, however. Luther, his coat stained with Forbes's blood, was posted in the yard, keeping watch. He was holding Carswell's shotgun, and he smiled up at Cody.

Phoebe was still in the barn, as far as Cody knew, but he really didn't want to think about what she was doing in there. He turned away from the window and looked around at the bedroom that was serving as their cell.

Unlike the bedroom Cody had been in, there wasn't a fireplace in this one, which meant that not only was it a bit cold in the room, there was no chance of trying to send anyone up the chimney. The Reverend Woodley was so small that he might've been able to scoot up inside a chimney and escape without being seen by Luther, but Carswell had probably thought of that, which was why they had been put in a room without a fireplace.

There was only one chair in the room, and Woodley had placed it near the window so that he could sit there and read his Bible. He was remarkably calm and appeared to take a great deal of comfort in the Scriptures.

Eli wasn't calm. He paced up and down the length of the small room, his wound apparently forgotten, every now and then muttering something under his breath. The gist of his remarks seemed to Cody to have something to do with Eli's amazement that he had ever planned to stay in such a place and had entertained romantic notions about the Carswell sisters.

Cody looked over at Hope. The only good thing about the current arrangement was that it gave them some time to talk. He walked over to where she was sitting on the bed and joined her.

Hope looked up at him and forced a tiny smile that didn't quite reach her blue eyes. "You don't look very happy about things," she remarked.

Cody grinned ruefully. "I'm just sorry that you got dragged into this."

"What do you mean by that? Are you thinking that because I'm a woman, I can't hold up? You should know by now that I'm not like Sue Beth or Nancy."

"I knew that a long time back," Cody said. "No, I meant I'm sorry you got dragged into it because I'd sure like to have gotten to know you better, and it doesn't seem like this is the place where that can happen."

"That sounds pretty promising," Hope said. "Or at least part of it does. Just how well would you like to get to know me?"

Cody put an arm around her, and she moved closer to him. "Better than I did the other night," he said, referring to the brief kiss they'd shared. "You're the first woman I've met in a long time who's made me think there's more to life than just being a lawman."

"Does the law really mean that much to you?"

"It sure does." Cody told her a little about his past, about his father's death and how it had been avenged, about the ranch where his mother and sisters still lived . . . private things that Cody had rarely told to anyone, not even to Marie Jermaine.

He realized that he had come to care as much for Hope as he did for Marie, but in an entirely different way—a way that made him actually think about someday getting married and settling down. He was filled with a bitter regret that any future they might've had seemed doomed by the Carswells.

"I thought that you were a little insolent at first," Hope told him. "I don't much like it when people make assumptions about me based on nothing more than my appearance."

"That's not a mistake I'm likely to repeat," Cody said dryly. "But it is a real pretty appearance, if you don't mind my saying so."

"I don't mind it at all, now that I've gotten to know you. I sort of like your appearance, too."

Cody looked over at Woodley, whose head was buried in his Bible, and at Eli, who was still pacing.

"I kind of wish they'd put those two in some other room," he said.

Hope gave him an impish grin. "Why? Are you bashful?"

"Nope," Cody said. "But you did say the other night that you needed to think some more about it before you got kissed again."

"I've thought about it."

"What did you decide?"

"I've decided that doing it again might be a very good idea."

"Then I'd be mighty pleased to oblige you," Cody said, and he did.

This time, Hope responded fully, and it was quite a while before Cody remembered where he was. The sound of Reverend Woodley very deliberately clearing his throat finally registered on Cody, and he slowly drew away from Hope and looked across the room.

Woodley sat in the chair holding his Bible in his right hand. The book was closed, but Woodley had marked his place by keeping his index finger between the pages.

"Young love is a fine thing, I guess, but you don't seem very concerned about our situation, Mr. Cody," Woodley said when he had the Ranger's attention. "Is there something you know that you haven't told the rest of us, or have you just forgotten where we are?"

Cody saw that Eli had stopped pacing and was waiting

for his answer. "Nope," he said. "I haven't forgotten a thing. I just found out that I'm as human as the next fella."

Woodley smiled. "So I noticed. But it might be better if you turned your attention to our situation and we applied ourselves to finding a way out of this mess."

Cody nodded at the Bible Woodley held. "I thought you were looking for a way out in the Scriptures."

"I believe in the Scriptures," Woodley said. "There's much comfort to be found there. But I also believe in action. It was Ben Franklin, as I recall, in his guise of Poor Richard, who said that the Lord helps those who help themselves."

"That's a mighty nice thought," Eli said, "but thoughts ain't goin' to make much difference to any of us if we wind up like poor Gus did."

"We're not going to wind up like Gus," Cody told him firmly. "We're going to help ourselves, just like Reverend Woodley said. I don't have any intention of letting the Carswells butcher me like a buck deer."

"Then like somethin' else the Reverend said, you must know somethin' that we don't," Eli remarked. "I sure wish I could be as relaxed as you are—and maybe I would if a fine woman like Dr. Baxter wanted me to kiss her—but I don't see much of a way out of this. Just how're we goin' to help ourselves?"

Woodley wanted to know the answer to that one, too. "Indeed," he said, "they have all our weapons, and I guess you've seen Luther standing down below the window there with the shotgun. Even if we could make some kind of rope out of the sheets on that bed, we couldn't get away. He'd kill us before we got to the ground."

"I've been thinking about that," Cody said, realizing that he was telling the truth, though if they'd asked him he couldn't have told them *when* he'd been thinking about it. He must've been, however, because the answer was right there in his head, and it must've come from somewhere. "About the weapons, I mean. They didn't take *all* the weapons."

Eli looked around the room dubiously. "You have better eyes than I do, then. I sure as hell don't see anything that looks like a gun in here."

"I didn't say anything about guns," Cody told him. "I said *weapons*."

"Don't see no weapons, either," Eli said, "unless you're thinkin' of breakin' up that chair and beatin' the Carswells to death with the legs."

Cody laughed. "That's not what I had in mind, but if worse comes to worst we might give it a try. But I've got a better idea. Remember what happened at your cabin when Gus and Rachel got the jump on us?"

Eli shook his head.

But Hope remembered. "My bag!" she said. "The scalpels in my bag!"

"There might be other things that we could use in there, too," Cody said.

"That's all well and good," Eli broke in. "But I don't see no doctor's bag, either."

"It must still be in my bedroom," Hope said. "Do you think they've taken it?"

Cody shook his head. "I doubt it. They wouldn't have any reason to. They probably haven't even thought about it."

"Then all we have to do is get hold of it," Hope said. "And figure out how to use what's in it. They might not let us have it, though."

"What about my wound?" Eli said.

"It's healing very well," Hope said. "It shouldn't give you any trouble."

Eli grinned wryly. "I don't reckon *nothin'* will be givin' me any trouble after tonight, if the Carswells have their way. What I meant was, could you tell 'em you need that bag to take care of me?"

Cody thought about that. "They might not fall for it. They know you're doing fine."

"What if I weren't?" Eli asked. "What if it started in to bleed again?"

"There's no reason that it should," Hope answered. "The healing process is proceeding normally."

"Wait a second," Cody said to Eli. "Are you suggesting that we *make* it bleed?"

Eli shrugged, trying to look casual. "If that's what it takes."

Hope didn't like the direction the conversation was heading. Her face stiffened. "I can't allow that. Eli is my patient, and I won't let you deliberately harm him."

"You're thinking like a doctor," Cody said. "You've got to start thinking like a prisoner. If we don't hurt Eli a little bit now, the Carswells are going to do a lot worse to him later on."

Hope saw his point. Her face relaxed somewhat. "I understand. All right. It might be all right to open his wound slightly. Even if they won't bring the bag, we can use the sheets to rebandage him."

"Good," Cody said. "Now why don't you tell us what you've got in that bag."

When it came right down to it, Eli plainly didn't relish the idea of opening his wound, but he stood by the chair where Woodley had sat, his hands gripping the back with all his might. He had a piece of sheet wadded in his mouth.

"Don't hit him too hard," Hope said. "We just want to start a little bleeding, not tear the whole thing open."

Eli pulled out the sheet. "That's a mighty comfortin' thought. You better go ahead, Cody, before I change my mind." He stuck the sheet back in his mouth, clamped down on it, and closed his eyes.

Cody hit him in the side with his balled fist. He tried to hit exactly where Hope had indicated, and he pulled the punch so that it wouldn't hit with its full force.

It hit hard enough, however. Eli gave a muffled groan and nearly collapsed against the chair. It was only a second before blood stained his bandage.

"Call her," Cody told Woodley, who was standing by the door. He took the piece of sheet from Eli's mouth and tossed it to Hope, who shoved it under the bed.

The preacher started pounding on the door and yelling for Diana.

"What's the trouble in there?" Diana asked through the door.

"It's Mr. Peyton," Woodley said. "His wound is bleeding again, and Dr. Baxter wants to treat it. She needs her medical bag."

They could hear Diana laughing through the door. "You people must be crazy. He's not going to live long enough to need any treatment."

Cody had already thought of an answer to that. "If he's not taken care of, he won't be able to come down to that big supper tonight. He'll miss the entertainment. And everyone is supposed to be there."

There was silence on the other side of the door for a moment. Then Diana said, "I guess you're right. Where's that bag?"

"In the bedroom where I was staying," Hope called.

"I'll get it," Diana said. "I'll be right back."

She was as good as her word. Within moments she was knocking on the door, saying, "I'm going to unlock the door now. When it swings open, I want to be able to see all of you on the other side of the room. Otherwise, I'll start shooting."

"Everybody move back from the door," Cody said.

Eli was already sitting in the chair. The others moved back so that Diana could have a good view of them.

"All right," Cody said. "We're clear of the door."

"You'd better be," Diana said.

The door swung inward. Diana stood framed in the doorway, covering the room with her pistol. The medical bag was on the floor by her feet. When she was satisfied that no one was going to try to jump her and that Eli was actually in need of assistance, she bent and picked up the black satchel, never taking her eyes off the occupants of the room.

"He doesn't look so good," she said, looking at Eli as she came through the door. "My father will be very displeased if he doesn't come down for supper." She glanced at Hope. "You can come over here and get your bag, Doctor." Then she waved the pistol at Cody and Woodley and instructed, "You two sit on the bed."

The Ranger and the preacher did as they were told. Hope crossed the room. Cody had warned her that Diana might think to check the bag's contents and to try to distract Diana's attention by talking to her.

"Thank you," Hope said, taking the bag. "It's kind of

you to let me attend my patient. I have to admit that I'm surprised you did."

"I don't want my father to be disappointed," Diana said. "You don't know what he's like when he's disappointed."

"I can well imagine," Hope said, turning away from Diana as she placed the bag on the floor by Eli. "It must be a terrible life."

"That's where you're wrong," Diana said. "It's a lot of fun. We live free, and we don't have any law trying to tell us what to do." She looked at Cody. "We don't hold much with the law."

Hope cut away Eli's bandage with a pair of scissors. "But look at you," she said, keeping up the steady chatter. "You're a smart, beautiful woman—as are all your sisters—yet you've chosen such an appalling way of life. What I don't understand is how you ever got started doing such terrible things."

Diana shrugged. "They're not so terrible. People slaughter animals. What we do isn't so different. As to how we got started, I couldn't tell you that. We've been doing it ever since I can remember."

Hope removed the soiled dressing and replaced it with a clean one. The wound had already stopped bleeding. Cody had done a good job of pulling his punch. Hope finished up and was about to put the scissors back in her bag.

"I'll take those," Diana said.

Hope handed them to her. "Very well. They aren't dangerous, you know."

Diana slipped the small scissors in a pocket without saying anything. Hope put the rest of the clean bandage in the satchel, packing it in neatly, and snapped it shut.

"I'll take the bag, too," Diana said.

Hope picked it up and handed it to her.

Diana indicated Eli. "He's going to be able to come to supper, isn't he?"

"What do you think, Eli?" Hope said.

Eli's voice was only a little strained. "Sure. I wouldn't miss it."

Diana nodded with satisfaction. "You'd better not." She looked at Cody and Woodley. "You'd all better be there."

"Do we have a choice?" Woodley asked coldly.

Diana grinned. "No," she said and left the room. They could hear her locking the door behind her.

They waited in silence for several minutes after they heard Diana's steps going down the hall. Finally, Cody asked, "Did you get it?"

For an answer, Hope shook her arm and let the scalpel slide into her hand. She held it out to him. He took it and slipped it inside his vest out of sight.

"Be careful," Hope warned him. "It's sharp."

"I hope so," Cody said grimly.

Eli looked at Hope with admiration. "I got to hand it to you, ma'am. If you weren't such a good doctor, you could get a job in a minute doin' tricks in a medicine show."

"What about the other stuff?" Cody said.

Hope shook her other sleeve, and a small glass vial slid into her hand. She held it up for them all to see.

"Are you sure that'll work?" Woodley asked. "It doesn't look like much."

"There's plenty," Hope said. "As I told you, it's a very powerful sedative. It should work if I get a chance to use it."

Eli was as curious about the potion as the preacher. "How much will it take?"

"A few drops would be enough in normal circumstances, but since we want fast action, I'll use all of it."

"Will it kill 'em?" Eli asked.

Hope wasn't sure, but the truth was that no one cared as long as it took at least one of the Carswells out of action.

"Now what?" Woodley asked.

"Now?" Cody said, looking at each of them. "Now I reckon we wait. Then we'll see what we can do with what we've got—and hope that'll be enough."

"And trust in the Lord," Woodley said.

"Yep," Cody said. "That, too."

CHAPTER
||||||||||||||||||||||||| **15** |||||||||||||||||||||||||

Hayden Carswell sat in the parlor while his daughters prepared the last supper for the prisoners. From the window he could see Luther standing guard in the yard with the shotgun. He would have to let his son come in soon and change his clothing. It would never do for anyone to attend the dinner in such a soiled outfit.

Carswell was proud of Luther, in a way. The boy had never been the comfort that his sisters had been after their mothers had died, of course, but he had done his best. It was too bad that he hadn't inherited something of the grace and beauty that the girls possessed, but he was strong and loyal, and those were qualities that Carswell valued.

His daughters, however, were his pride and joy. All four had different mothers because it seemed that none of the women Carswell had married or lived with had ever quite been able to adjust to some of his more peculiar habits. Two of them had even threatened to inform the law about his activities, which at that time were hardly anything to compare to what he'd been able to accomplish when he had grown children to help him. It was too bad that his wives had threatened him. By doing so they had practically begged him to dispose of them, a chore that he didn't regret as much as they must have supposed he might.

In fact, Elizabeth, his third wife, was the first he had butchered and preserved. That had been in Nebraska, where cold winters were much more frequent than they were in Texas. To tell the truth, Carswell and his family had preserved very few travelers until the present storm. The weather simply hadn't cooperated.

They had killed quite a few, however, and taken what they possessed. There hadn't been that many until the Carswells discovered their present house only a little more than a year previously. It had proved practically an ideal base of operations, and they had settled in gratefully. If only the winters in that part of Texas had been colder it would have been perfect.

In hindsight, it was too bad that they had saved the Ranger, Carswell thought. It would've been better to let him die where he'd fallen, but they hadn't been thinking clearly. Now there was a distinct possibility that other Rangers would come looking for the man they had lost.

What he regretted most about that was the fact that he wouldn't be able to kill the ones who came. To do so would be to ensure his own doom, and Carswell wasn't ready for that. He intended to live where he was for years, preying on any unwary traveler who happened by.

So when the Rangers came, he'd simply lie to them. He would tell them about coming upon a mortally wounded man and his already-dead companions, a beautiful blond female and a darkly tanned man in his midthirties. He would explain that the man, who had identified himself as Cody, had told of being set upon by a band of outlaws, now long gone, who had come to free their friend— Cody's prisoner. And he would express his deep regrets that he had, tragically, arrived too late to be of any help.

He would show them the graves where Cody and the others were buried, and if the Rangers wanted to dig up the bodies and return them to Del Rio, he wouldn't try to stop them.

For there would be bodies in the graves, complete with their valuables. Carswell would see to it. The unfortunate part of making the facts fit the lie was that doing so would take a great deal of the fun out of disposing of Cody and Dr. Baxter and Eli Peyton. He would have to see to it that they were simply shot, as they would have been by the outlaws.

But as for the pious Woodley and his flock, they could be disposed of in ways that would bring a great deal of pleasure to the Carswells. That would have to be satisfaction enough.

The thought of it made Hayden Carswell smile. He got up from his chair. It was time to allow Luther to get dressed for dinner.

Cody glanced out the bedroom window. The sun was sinking below the horizon, and the sky burned a brilliant orange-red. It was going to be a clear, cold night.

There was still light in the sky when a knock sounded at the door.

"Come on in," the Ranger called, with a fair attempt at good spirits.

There was the sound of a key turning in the lock, and then the door opened. Francesca stood there, dressed in a beautiful green satin gown that set off to perfection her creamy skin and the red hair piled high on her head. A gold necklace glittered around her neck, and a carved ivory locket dangled from it.

The dress was cut low and revealed a wide expanse of shoulder and bosom. The only thing that ruined the effect was the .32 caliber revolver she held in her right hand.

Cody was impressed with her beauty in spite of himself. It was hard to believe that someone so lovely could be so evil, and he had to remind himself again of the dangers of judging by appearances. Of course, the revolver wasn't misleading at all. It told the whole truth and nothing but.

"Sorry about our clothes," Cody said with mock humility. All of them wore traveling clothes that were by now a little the worse for wear. "We didn't know we were supposed to dress up."

"That's all right," Francesca said, taking his remark seriously. "You're guests, so you don't have to dress. You shouldn't let it make you feel uncomfortable."

Cody had to suppress a laugh. Did she really think they'd feel uncomfortable about their clothes when they were being set up for a killing?

"If you'll walk ahead of me, please . . ." Francesca said politely.

Cody thought for a moment that now might be the time to make a break for it. She could shoot one, maybe two, of them before they overpowered her, but by then they'd have a pistol and a hostage.

"Diana's standing out there in the hall," Francesca said, as if sensing exactly what Cody was thinking. "She has a pistol, too, so I'd advise you not to try anything."

"Never gave it a thought," Cody lied. "I'm mighty hungry, myself. I wouldn't want to miss supper."

He went out into the hallway, followed by the others. Sure enough, Diana, her pistol at the ready, was standing only a few feet down the hall. She was dressed just as elegantly as her sister, though her dress was black—which Cody thought a much more appropriate color for the evening than the one Francesca wore.

The Prescotts and the Evanses—watched over by a pistol-toting Phoebe—were at the head of the stairs, looking quite unhappy while waiting for the others. Kept in tight ranks by the sisters, the prisoners all marched downstairs and filed into the dining room, which was done up more elaborately than it had been on any previous evening. When Carswell had promised them that he would give as good as he got, Cody thought, he hadn't been lying—at least not from his point of view.

The room was brilliantly lit by a kerosene-filled chandelier above the table, which was spread with a dazzlingly white damask cloth. Sitting on the cloth were cut-crystal goblets, plates of hand-painted bone china, and eating utensils of fine silver, all of which caught the light and caused it to sparkle and shine around the room.

Arrayed around the table were uncovered bowls of green beans, a large bowl of mashed potatoes, and several loaves of fresh bread. At the head of the table sat a big roast on a platter and a gravy boat filled to the top. There were even two apple pies sitting on the sideboard, steam rising from slits in their fluffy crusts. Several crystal decanters of red wine added color to the table, and wine had been poured into stemmed glasses at each place. It all looked good—though it would have looked much more appetizing in the Rio Grande Hotel, Cody decided.

The Ranger was impressed. Say what you wanted to about the Carswells—and they were undoubtedly as crazy as a cayuse that had eaten nothing but locoweed for a month—they knew how to set a table.

And even more striking than the table were the Carswells themselves. Like their sisters, Phoebe and Brenna were elegantly groomed and gowned, in red and blue respectively, and the sight of the four sisters together was almost enough to make a man's knees go weak on him. It was a hell of a waste of beauty and womanhood, if you asked Cody. He heard Eli let out a regretful sigh, and he figured that the rancher was feeling the same way.

Even Luther was well turned out. His hair was neatly combed, and it looked as if his beard had been trimmed. He was wearing a heavy gray suit that was only slightly too small for him—Luther strained the shoulders, and his bare wrists stuck out about an inch from the coat sleeves—but Cody had to forgive him for that. Probably no traveler who'd been unlucky enough to stumble on the Carswells had owned a suit that fit Luther.

Carswell himself was standing behind his chair at the head of the table. He was wearing a black cutaway coat and pants, with a black vest, white shirt, and black tie. A gold watch chain was draped across the vest. He looked uncomfortably like an undertaker to Cody, all too fitting and proper under the circumstances.

To Carswell's right was Rachel, and the transformation that had been worked on her was practically astounding. Cody had never seen her wearing anything except jeans and boots and a man's shirt and coat. Someone—the sisters, no doubt—had cleaned her up, fixed her hair, and furnished her with a white dress the equal of any that they were wearing. She looked so young and innocent that Cody thought she could have passed for some socialite's daughter in San Antonio. He didn't much blame Carswell for taking her into the family; she was not only very pretty, she had the morals of a rattler.

Francesca walked the length of the table and took the place beside Rachel. Diana took the chair opposite her. It was clear then that the sisters had taken in Rachel and accepted her, even Francesca. Cody was sure that Carswell could be mighty convincing when he wanted to be.

The patriarch welcomed his "guests," as he insisted on referring to them, and apologized for having kept them locked up all day. "But then, we wouldn't have wanted you to miss this meal, and we weren't sure that you'd stay around if we gave you the opportunity to roam about."

That remark got a smile from Rachel and the sisters and a hoarse laugh from Luther.

Carswell waved a hand at the table, "And now, Mr. Cody, what do you think of our hospitality?"

"I never saw anything to beat it," Cody said truthfully. It was pretty clear that the Carswells had profited mightily from their brutal crimes.

Carswell seemed pleased with Cody's answer. "And you, Dr. Baxter?"

"It's beautiful," Hope said.

"Reverend Woodley?"

Woodley's eyes burned with the light of a man who was confronting Satan himself. "The feast of the golden calf. The worship of Mammon. The—"

"That's enough of that," Carswell interrupted. "You're as tiresome a man as I ever let stay under my roof. What about you, Mr. Peyton?"

"I live in a one-room cabin," Eli said. "I never saw anything like this."

That answer was more to Carswell's liking. The Prescotts and the Evanses said nothing, but he interpreted their silence as concurrence and said, "I'm glad you all like it. Except you, of course, Mr. Woodley. I would request that you honor us by asking a blessing, but I'm afraid you might start sermonizing again. So I think it would be best for all of us to sit down and enjoy our meal without the benefit of grace. But first, let's have a toast."

Carswell picked up his wineglass and held it high. Cody didn't see any need to hesitate, and he took up his as well. Soon everyone was ready.

"To our guests," Carswell said. "And to the bounty that we share." After everyone had taken a sip of their wine, Carswell said, "And now, everyone, please sit."

There was a general scraping of chairs, and Cody pulled out Hope's chair for her, but before anyone could sit, Eli spoke up. "I hate to say this," he announced, "but I just don't know if I can eat, thinkin' about Gus and all." He met Carswell's eyes. "I mean, it's bad enough to know he's dead, but after what you said this mornin' . . . well, I wouldn't want to eat anything that I didn't know what it was."

Carswell smiled thinly. "You have an even lower opinion of me than I thought, Mr. Peyton. Let me assure you that I would never ask my guests to eat the food that my family and I sometimes partake of. It isn't a matter of routine with us, although I think you might like it if you could get over your stupid prejudices." He looked at the platter in front of him. "However, this is nothing more than good Texas beef, as you will know as soon as you taste it. Now, please sit down."

Everyone sat. Carswell carved the roast and passed the plates to his "guests." The only sound was the clinking of silverware against china and the tinkle of glass against glass as the laden dinner plates were set down by the bread plates.

When Carswell was finished with the carving, he began talking to Rachel, and soon the sisters were talking as well. The guests, however, had little to say, though Cody thought they were doing very well at pretending to be having a dignified dinner when in actuality they were simply marking time until the Carswells put them to death. Cody wondered how the family planned to do it. And would they change clothes before they went about their grisly task? It would be a shame to mess up their fine attire, but maybe they didn't care much about that. Maybe there were plenty more clothes where those had come from.

Not that he was going to wait to find out. He was going to enjoy his meal, of course, and he hoped the others would as well. They needed the food, because none of them had eaten since the night before. But if Carswell thought that Cody was going to sit around meekly and let the end come without a fight, he was dead wrong.

When the main course was over and the dinner plates removed, Diana went around the table pouring dessert wine. Phoebe and Brenna followed their sister, handing each diner a dessert plate filled with a generous slice of pie. Cody was sitting next to Hope, and he nudged her foot under the table with the toe of his boot. She nodded imperceptibly, and Cody dug into his pie, which turned out to be as delicious as the rest of the meal had been. It was really too bad about the Carswells, he thought. At least one of them was a really good cook.

Suddenly Hope stood up, shoving back her chair. "I can't stand this any longer!" she shrieked, looking wildly at Cody and then at the Reverend Woodley. "I don't see how you can sit here so calmly, knowing that they're going to kill all of us as soon as we're finished! Well, I don't want to die!"

She rushed down the table, stopping beside Luther, who looked at her with surprise. "Please," she begged. "Please! You've got to save me! You can't let them kill me!"

Luther looked embarrassed and tried to push her away.

"No!" Hope cried. "Think about it. Your father has a lover. Look at her there, dressed in white like a virgin bride! But who is there for you? Your sisters had their fun with Mr. Forbes, but who were you allowed to enjoy?"

Luther wasn't trying to push her away anymore. He was looking at his father, who was watching with interest. Sue Beth Prescott and Nancy Evans looked on in horror, their mouths open in amazement. Cody could tell that they'd rather die than let Luther touch them. He didn't much blame them.

"Look at me," Hope implored Luther. "Don't you think I'm pretty?"

Luther licked his lips. "Yeah," he said. "Yeah."

"I could make you very happy, Luther," Hope said seductively. "You wouldn't be sorry. You'd see what I can do for a man."

She insinuated herself between Luther and the table and tried to wriggle her way into his lap.

"This has gone far enough," Carswell boomed. "Dr. Baxter, leave my son alone and return to your seat at once."

"No!" Hope said, throwing her arms around Luther's neck. "No! I don't want to die!"

Luther eyed his father. Cody thought he looked a bit like a faithful dog who wanted his master to throw him a bone.

"No, Luther," Carswell said firmly. "It's not possible. We've taken in one outsider, and that's more than enough. We won't be taking in another."

"That's because you got the one we took in," Luther said, surprising Cody considerably. He'd thought that "yeah" was the only word Luther knew. "You don't ever want me to have anything," Luther continued. "You keep me upstairs, out of sight. I always miss most of the fun. It's not fair."

"Listen, boy," Carswell said threateningly, "are you trying to tell me how to take care of my own family?"

Cody noticed that the sisters were watching this confrontation with eager eyes. It seemed likely that Luther didn't often challenge Carswell's authority; maybe it had never happened before, and the sisters were just as interested as everyone else in seeing how things would turn out.

"No," Luther said, "I'm not tellin' you that. I'm just sayin' that it seems like you and the girls have all the fun, and I'm stuck out in the barn or upstairs all by myself. I don't see why I can't have a little company."

"You wouldn't be sorry," Hope said, fluttering her lashes at him. "I'd make you very happy."

Carswell stood up, gripping his napkin hard in his fist. "Dr. Baxter, I'm going to ask you once more to return to your seat. I don't want to have to ruin dinner. But if you don't go, and go now, I'm afraid you won't be around to finish your dessert."

"You don't mean that you'd kill me right now," Hope said. "Not at dinner!"

"*I* wouldn't kill you," Carswell said. "But Luther would if I asked him to. Wouldn't you, Luther?"

Luther didn't say anything. He looked down at Hope's blue eyes, and then he looked at his father.

"Wouldn't you, Luther?" Carswell demanded.

Luther stared at Carswell for several seconds. At first Cody saw a flicker of defiance, but then Luther dropped his eyes, not looking at Hope, but at the wineglass in front of him.

"Yeah," he said finally. "Yeah."

Hope was beaten. She whimpered softly and got out of Luther's lap. Then she drew herself up slowly, dried her eyes with the napkin that she'd been holding, and walked back to her seat.

"You can see that my family understands the meaning of loyalty," Carswell said.

Or of fear, more likely, Cody thought. He wondered how often and in what ways Luther had been punished to make him so obedient to his father's will.

Hope sat down beside Cody, her eyes downcast, but she tipped him a wink to let him know that she had managed to dump the contents of the sedative vial into Luther's wine.

Eli was right, Cody thought. She really was good, *very* good. He hadn't seen her do it, and he'd been watching the whole time. If they got out of this mess he'd have to remember to ask her just where she'd learned her sleight-of-hand skills.

Luther was still upset by what had happened, and Cody could tell that the young man was resentful of his father's handling of things. That was fine with Cody, especially since to cover his resentment Luther grabbed his wineglass and drank the contents down in one long gulp. Even if the sedative had given a bitter flavor to the wine, Luther wouldn't have noticed, thanks to his anger and to the speed with which he swallowed the liquid.

Cody finished off his pie, keeping a close watch on Luther out of the corner of his eye, expecting the big man to keel over at any second.

It didn't happen. After a few minutes, Cody began to get worried. Luther was apparently unaffected by the drug. He was sitting in his chair gobbling pie as if the doctored wine he'd consumed had been no more potent than well water.

Cody looked questioningly at Hope, but all she could do was give a slight shrug. He wondered if maybe the drug was old and had lost its potency, but he couldn't ask. One of the Carswells might overhear him.

Another minute went by and still nothing happened. Cody thought then that they had made a mistake in making Luther their target. He was so huge that the drug might not affect him as quickly or as completely as it would a person of normal size. It was like trying to drug an ox.

But it was too late to consider that now, and there really hadn't been any other choice. It would've looked pretty strange if he or Eli had tried to coax one of the women the way Hope had worked on Luther, and neither Cody nor Eli was as quick of hand as Hope. They'd most likely have been unable to slip the sedative into a glass undetected as Hope had done.

Carswell finished the last crumbs of his pie, pushed his plate back, touched his napkin to the corner of his mouth, and looked down the table. Cody knew that the time had come for the family to put into effect whatever plan they had for disposing of their guests, and he wondered how he was going to be able to use the scalpel he had concealed in his vest. He'd been counting on Luther to provide a distraction, but Luther wasn't cooperating.

Cody looked at the Carswell sisters. Phoebe was nearest him. It might be possible for him to reach her before her sisters could get to the pistols they had hidden somewhere under their gowns, though he doubted it. There were too many people between him and her. The other women would probably put several shots into him before he reached her. Nevertheless, it looked like the only chance they had, and he could feel his muscles begin to tense for the effort.

He was about to make his move when Luther moved first. He stood suddenly upright, kicking his chair backward so hard that it crashed into the wall and fell over.

"Luther!" Carswell exclaimed, his eyes wide with shock. "What's the matter, son?"

This was the distraction that Cody had been waiting for, and he was on the move instantly. No one even noticed him. They were all too busy staring at Luther, whose reaction, now that it had finally come, was more than Cody could have hoped for.

Luther stood as straight as a tree while a shudder shook his massive frame. He opened his mouth and tried to speak, but only a sort of croaking sound emerged. His large hands went to his throat and began tearing at his collar. He ripped the collar off and threw it aside, and the top button of his shirt popped across the table and pinged off the gravy boat. His face was suffused with blood and colored a dark, unhealthy red.

His sisters stared at him with a dreadful fascination.

"Luther!" Carswell shouted.

"A-a-rrrrrrrr," Luther said.

Then his eyes rolled up in his head and he fell face forward onto the table, smashing plates and sending silverware and glasses flying. His head struck with a solid thud, and he slid slowly backward off the table and disappeared from sight.

"Dr. Baxter!" Carswell said. "See what's happen—"

His words were cut off when Cody grabbed a fistful of his hair from behind, jerked his head back, and pressed the keen edge of the scalpel against his neck.

The sisters had been staring at the spot where Luther had disappeared from, but their heads snapped around at the sudden cessation of their father's voice.

Cody was amazed at the speed with which the pistols appeared in their hands. He wasn't even sure where the guns had come from—did ball gowns have pockets? he wondered—but each sister held one. Phoebe and Diana held theirs on the other guests while Francesca and Brenna tried to train theirs on Cody, who kept himself well concealed behind their father.

"Put the pistols on the floor," Cody ordered. "If you don't, I'll slice him open and drain him just like you did Gus. But I won't be quite so neat."

There was silence as the sisters tried to decide what to do. For just a second Cody could hear Luther squirming around on the floor under the table, and then even that sound stopped.

"Put the pistols down *now*," Cody ordered. He drew the tip of the scalpel along Carswell's neck, producing an inch-long thin red line. "I don't have any reason to keep him alive."

"You've already killed Luther, you son of a bitch," Francesca said.

"He's not dead," Cody told her. "Not yet. But your father will be if you don't get rid of those guns."

Rachel, who hadn't said a word, now made a jump at Cody. He twisted slightly to the side and planted a boot solidly in her stomach, sending her flying away from the table. Her head hit the wall with a loud crack, and she slid down to the floor.

Cody had exposed just enough of himself to give Francesca a target, and he heard the explosion of the pistol. The bullet whined past as he quickly twisted back around, thrusting Carswell in front of him.

"I told you to put the guns down," Cody said. "Now I'm going to kill him."

"We'll kill you for sure if you do," Francesca said. "And all your friends, too."

"Maybe," Cody admitted. "And maybe you can hang us all out there in the barn with the others. But you can for damn sure hang your father out there along with us. Who'll you eat first?" He sank the point of the scalpel into Carswell's throat and blood spurted out in a slender stream.

"Wait!" Phoebe cried. "We'll put the guns down. You wait!"

Phoebe, Diana, and Brenna bent down and laid their pistols on the floor, but Francesca stared at Cody defiantly. She didn't make a move.

A crooked smile appeared on Carswell's face, and a mad gleam was in his eyes. "You were always the one most like me, Francesca," he said. "Shoot him!"

"I can't," she said miserably. "I'll hit you."

"That doesn't matter. The family must be protected. You have to kill him. Shoot him even if you have to shoot through me."

Francesca's mouth tightened with determination, but she didn't pull the trigger. "I . . . I can't," she said. "I don't want to kill you."

Carswell tried to draw himself up, but he was held too tightly in Cody's grip to do so. Nevertheless, his voice rang out in the room.

"Do as your father tells you, Francesca!" he commanded.

Francesca gathered her nerve, and her finger tightened on the trigger.

During the byplay between Carswell and Francesca, the Reverend Woodley had been slowly making his way unseen down the side of the table behind everyone's back. It was apparent that this time Francesca was going to fire, and it was too late to do anything else, so Woodley threw himself forward in front of Carswell just as Francesca pulled the trigger.

The pistol crashed, and the bullet struck Woodley hard in his upper body.

He pitched onto the table. His head struck the platter containing what remained of the roast, sending it over the side of the table to the floor, where it dumped its contents and splintered into fragments.

Cody had never intended to slit Carswell's throat. He was too much of a lawman to kill even a monster like Hayden Carswell in cold blood. Now he jerked the scalpel aside and slammed a fist into the back of Carswell's head. As Carswell fell forward, Cody grabbed the man's pistol and pulled it from its holster.

Then everything went to hell all at once.

CHAPTER
||||||||||||||||||||| 16 |||||||||||||||||||||

Before Cody could fire the pistol, Carswell, stunned from the blow to his head but strengthened with the frenzy of madness, whirled around and attacked the Ranger like some kind of crazed beast. His lips were stretched tight in an insane rictus that exposed his teeth to the gum line. He flailed his arms about wildly, striking Cody repeatedly, and though he wasn't doing much damage, he was able to keep Cody from using the pistol. Cody didn't dare pull the trigger for fear of hitting the wrong person in the crowded room if the pistol was knocked off line.

Francesca had no such fears, and she fired the .32 again, but the shot missed Cody, thanks to Eli, who had flung himself onto her back like a sack of hog feed, bearing her to the floor. She lost the pistol in the fall, but she twisted under Eli and raked his cheek with her fingernails and then hit him in his wound with her elbow.

Tears popped into Eli's eyes as he yelped in pain, but he got a grip on Francesca's hair and banged her head into the floor again and again. Finally she went limp, and Eli felt around for the pistol she had dropped. His fingers closed on it, and he was standing up when Phoebe, having snatched up her own pistol, took a shot at him. Ducking back down under the table, he dropped Francesca's pistol, but Phoebe's bullet thudded harmlessly into the wall behind him.

Kenneth Prescott, waking up to the fact that if he acted fast he might be able to save himself and his wife, slammed a fist into Phoebe's wrist, knocking the pistol out of her hand. She dived after it, but Prescott kicked it away, and then he kicked Phoebe.

William Evans, taking his cue from Prescott, wrestled with Diana on the floor for possession of the gun she had placed there earlier. For just a second he thought about how unseemly it was for a religious man to be tangled in the arms and legs of a beautiful woman who wasn't his wife, but Diana kneed him in the groin and drove any such concerns from his head. He struggled with her just as hard as he'd have struggled with a man, and he didn't give another thought to her femininity.

Rachel, just now recovering from her collision with the wall, shook her head and looked around at the tumult raging in the room. Chairs were being overturned and bodies were hurtling about like leaves in a hurricane. Her eyes fastened on Cody and Carswell, and she got to her feet to help the man she had chosen—but Hope cut her off before she could reach him.

"Get out of my way, bitch!" Rachel snarled.

She threw a fist that struck the doctor in the side of the head, but Hope stood her ground and swung a hard right to Rachel's stomach. Hope's fist was small, but her arm was powerful enough to knock the air from Rachel, who staggered backward to the wall once more. Almost before she could catch her breath, Hope was on her.

Rachel reached up with both hands and grabbed Hope's blond hair. Pulling as hard as she could, she slammed Hope's head into the wall.

Diana was proving to be a lot stronger than she looked. Evans tried to get a grip on her, but she twisted away and snatched the pistol. She hit him in the face with it, and as he grappled with her, she fired wildly.

Her first bullet shattered the gravy boat and sent a brown spray over the tablecloth and over Liam Woodley, who still lay there without moving.

Her second shot almost took off the top of Eli's head as he tried once more to stand up. He ducked down again just in time to have a rejuvenated Francesca claw at his eyes. He slammed her on the point of the chin, and she subsided again.

Diana's third shot clipped the chain that supported the chandelier. The gleaming chandelier looked like a light-

ning bolt as it fell, and the result was much the same as
if a bolt had struck the house. Flaming kerosene spewed
all over the room.

Evans finally succeeded in knocking the pistol from
Diana's hand, thanks to her surprise at what she'd done.
He shoved her aside, got up, and grabbed his wife's
hand.

"Come on!" he yelled. "We're getting out of here!"

"What about the others?" Nancy asked tremulously. "It
isn't right to leave them behind."

"They're on their own. If we stay here, we'll be fried
like bacon. Come on!"

Nancy didn't hesitate any longer. She let him pull her
along toward the front door.

Prescott saw them going. He looked around for Sue
Beth, who was crouching down behind her chair, her eyes
tightly shut. He dragged her to her feet.

"Time to leave," he said.

"Yes!" she squealed. "Yes!" She clamped her fingers
around her husband's hand and followed him. She didn't
ask about the others; she didn't even open her eyes.

Within seconds after the chandelier fell the tablecloth
was burning, the walls were on fire, and Luther had
become a human torch. The fiery liquid had spilled all
over his upper body as he lay unconscious on the floor,
and it proved remarkably effective in reviving him.

He stood up with a frightful scream, his coat in flames,
and he raged through the room as he tried to tear the
coat off.

Cody had never really thought much about what Hell
might be like, but in that moment he reckoned he had a
pretty good idea.

The fire was spreading rapidly, flames blazing across
the floor and up the walls. Bodies thrashed all around,
and lurid shadows danced on the burning walls, as if a
giant was afire and running amuck. Meanwhile, Rachel
was trying to pound Hope's head to pudding, and if all
that wasn't enough, Cody had a maniac trying to beat the
life out of him.

He clubbed at Carswell's head with the pistol, opening
a bleeding gash on the madman's forehead, but Carswell

just laughed at him and grabbed at the gun. Cody tried to jerk it out of the way, but Carswell closed a hand on it and pulled his adversary forward. Then he butted Cody in the face.

Momentarily stunned, Cody lost his grip on the pistol and fell to the floor. Carswell, still laughing, aimed the pistol at him.

Luther, still trying to whip the burning rags of the coat off, collided with his father just at that instant, knocking the gun from his hand. Carswell stumbled forward and fell on top of Cody, who locked his hands around the killer's throat. He squeezed with all his might. Carswell's body went into convulsions. His hands beat at Cody's head, and the toes of his boots thundered like drumbeats on the wooden floor.

Smoke was filling the room now, but down on the floor where Cody was the air was still breathable. He took a deep breath and rolled over on top of Carswell, maintaining his hold on Carswell's neck. Cody would've tightened his grip if that'd been possible, but he was holding so tight already that it wasn't. Carswell was trying to talk or scream, it was impossible to tell which, but Cody's grasp was so strong that no sound escaped Carswell's mouth.

The Ranger could no longer see what was happening, but he could hear the crackling of the flames, the sounds of struggling, the occasional oaths of pain. He tried not to pay any attention to them. He blocked everything from his mind and held on to Carswell's throat for what seemed like an eternity. Finally, though, Carswell was no longer fighting. He was no longer moving at all.

His mouth was still open, but now his tongue bulged from it, and his eyes protruded grotesquely. The monster in human form was at last dead.

Cody shoved the body aside and stood up. It was hard to see in the smoke-filled room, but he could make out Eli leaning against the wall nearby, holding his side.

"Where is everybody?" Cody called.

Eli coughed for a second and then cleared his throat. "The Prescotts and Evanses cleared out."

Cody strained his eyes, trying to peer through the haze. He could see the Carswell sisters making their way to where their father lay dead. Their hair drooped in unruly ringlets around their faces, and their elaborate gowns were ripped and smeared.

"What about Hope?" he asked Eli.

"Luther got her," Eli said. "Took her upstairs, I think. He was headed thataway."

"Goddammit!" Cody snapped.

"Yeah," Eli said. "We gotta get out o' here."

"I'm not leaving Hope," Cody told him. He looked at the table where Woodley lay. The flames were licking at the preacher's clothes. "You get Woodley out if you can manage it. He may still be alive. I'm going after Hope."

Eli didn't ask any questions, just grabbed Woodley under the arms and dragged him off the table. He was limping badly because of his wound, but within seconds he had disappeared with the preacher through the smoke.

Luther had never experienced anything like the pain he was feeling now. It was as if his brain had been set on fire rather than his body. He wanted to scream and scream, but he didn't dare make a sound. His father wanted him to keep himself a secret. That was what he always said. *"You mustn't let them see you, Luther. They'd be afraid of you, and that would ruin everything. So you have to keep very quiet and stay out of sight."*

Luther had always done what his father told him to, at least about keeping quiet and staying out of sight, and he wasn't going to stop now.

He could keep quiet. He was good at that. He clamped his teeth together, and the screams that wanted to come out died somewhere inside him.

He could stay out of sight, too. There was no reason for anyone to see him ever again. He was willing to stay up on the third floor forever, since he was going to have company from now on.

That was one way he *would* disobey his father, who wasn't going to like that a bit, Luther knew, and he was a little afraid of what was going to happen to him. Still, that hadn't stopped him from grabbing Hope and carrying her up the stairs.

In some recess of his pain-warped mind Luther knew that the house was burning. He knew that his sisters and his father were down below him fighting for their lives, but he had wiped all that out of his consciousness. As much as he was suffering, he had long been denied something that he wanted, and now he was going to have it—and that thought drove everything else from his head. Taking Hope up to the third floor where they could live together forever was all that mattered to him.

When he reached the top of the stairs the door was locked. He had no idea where the key was, but that didn't make any difference. He raised his right leg and kicked the door off its hinges. Shouldering the fallen door out of his way, he went down the hallway to the second door on the right, which stood open. His room.

The bed was unmade, the bedclothes tangled and filthy. The floor was littered with dirty clothes, and the air had a sour odor.

None of that bothered Luther in the least. To him, it was home.

He laid Hope on the bed and looked at himself in the cracked mirror. He had left a lamp burning in the room when he'd dressed for dinner, and what he saw in its glimmering light almost caused him to let out the scream he was managing to keep inside. He had to grind his teeth so hard that he almost crushed them.

His shoulders and chest were terribly burned. Huge blisters were already forming there. His neck was burned, too, and the lower part of his face. Tears welled out of Luther's eyes, and he turned away from the mirror as he remembered what had happened downstairs. It was all his father's fault. If Luther had been allowed to take the woman with him in the first place, none of it would've happened. He realized that he'd left his family in a terrible situation, but he didn't care what happened to them now. Whatever it was, they deserved it. They'd had their fun through the years, and he'd always been the one left out. Let them see how they liked it.

He looked at Hope. He deserved her as his reward just as much as his family deserved their own fate. They should've let him have a woman before. But he was going to have one now, and there was nothing they could do to stop him.

His hand was loosening his belt as he moved toward the bed.

The old house was built strong, and if the wood was dry, it was also thick and hard, Cody thought as he climbed the stairs to the second floor. He figured that he had a few minutes at least before the flames worked their way up to wherever Luther had taken Hope.

The way he saw it, he had two problems. One of them was Luther. Cody had to find Carswell's son and get Hope away from him. The latter part wasn't going to be easy. Luther wasn't likely just to give in and smile and hand her over without a fight. The other problem was the house. Cody was afraid the whole place would collapse beneath him before he could find Hope and persuade Luther to give her up.

There was a third problem, too. Cody wasn't going to worry about that one until the time came, but he thought about it, nonetheless: Getting upstairs wasn't hard, since the fire hadn't spread there yet—but getting down again might prove to be tricky. Fires usually found stairways just as convenient as people did. The smoke was already swirling around him, stinging his eyes and burning in his lungs. He tried not to breathe too deeply.

When he reached the second-floor landing, he hesitated, but then he started up again. He wouldn't waste time searching there. He reckoned that Luther was hurting mighty bad, and he'd instinctively head for the third floor like a wounded animal would head for its den.

He hated to think what Luther might do to Hope up there.

His heels pounded on the stairs as he forced himself to run faster.

Hope opened her eyes and looked around, trying to figure out where she was. She had a fierce headache, and her vision was hazy. She blinked her eyes, and then things started to come back to her.

The last thing she remembered clearly was her fight with Rachel, who had practically beaten Hope's brains out against the wall until Hope, adopting the tactics of her adversary, had grasped Rachel's hair and tried to twist her head off.

Rachel's head hadn't come off, but she had been distracted from what she was doing to Hope. She had screamed and released Hope, who remembered getting halfway up and putting a knee into Rachel's face, letting go of her hair just before the knee connected.

There'd been a crack like breaking wood, and Rachel's head had snapped back and hit something. Hope couldn't remember what because when she had looked up, she saw Luther coming at her. The sight of him had taken her mind completely off Rachel. She'd turned to run, but Luther had swatted her with the back of one giant hand, knocking her out.

She'd been in the burning dining room when all that happened, but she obviously wasn't there now. Had Cody rescued her and taken her somewhere else?

The room was dimly lit, and she could see a dresser and chair. She realized that she was on a bed, and she smelled the sour sheets. Then she smelled the smoke.

A noise beside the bed made her turn her head. Luther, or what was left of him, was towering over her, his hand working at his belt.

She didn't waste time screaming. Instead, she rolled off the bed, hit the floor, and ran for the door.

Luther grabbed her by the neck and flung her back to the bed, then threw himself on top of her. She clawed at the ruined skin of his face, feeling it crackle and peel off under her fingernails.

This time Luther threw back his head and let the scream escape.

Hope wriggled out from under him, slipped off the bed, and headed for the door again.

Luther bit off his scream and leapt after her. He caught her before she reached the door, snatching the back of her shirt. The shirt tore as she wrenched herself away from him, exposing a wide area of her white skin. Luther screamed again, but this time in ecstasy.

He grabbed her belt and pulled her to him, turning her around quickly and pressing her arms to her sides so that she couldn't claw him again. There was blood streaming from his face, but he was trying to smile as he bent to kiss her.

Hope turned her head away in disgust and bit him hard on the arm, tearing at the burned flesh with her teeth. The sensation made her gag, and she felt that she was almost as much a cannibal as the Carswells. But Luther yelled in pain and released her.

Once more she turned for the door; once more Luther caught her before she got there. This time he didn't take any chances with her. He slammed her face with a ham-sized hand and knocked her to the floor. When she tried to get up, he hit her again. She didn't have the strength to make another try. He took her by the arm, dragged her to the bed, and threw her on the grubby sheets.

He clubbed her with his fist one more time. She bounced once and then sank back on the bed, unconscious.

CHAPTER
▬▬▬▬▬▬▬ 17 ▬▬▬▬▬▬▬

Francesca knelt over the body of her father, shaking his shoulders and imploring him to wake up. The smoke was nearly strangling her, and the heat of the fire was singeing her dress, but she felt strangely disconnected from those things. All she knew was that she couldn't leave her father there. He had always been the one who told them what to do, ever since they were children, and they had always obeyed him. He had to wake up and tell them what to do now.

Her sisters were gathered around the body with her, all of them talking softly to their father, desperately trying to awaken him from his deep sleep. It was simply inconceivable to them that he could be dead.

"Get up," Phoebe begged. "Please get up, Father. We can't stay here much longer."

"Don't just lie there," Diana said impatiently, choking as she inhaled the thick smoke. "You know that we have to get out of here right now! We have to find Luther. He's gone off somewhere with that woman, and you know we can't have her staying here. It would ruin everything."

Brenna was crying. "You've got to help us. That lawman got away. What if he brings more Rangers and they see the men in the barn? What will we tell them?"

There was, naturally enough, no reaction at all from Hayden Carswell.

"Can we leave him here, Francesca?" Phoebe asked in despair. "I don't think he hears us."

"Don't be a fool," Francesca snapped. "Of course we

can't leave him here. He'll wake up." She shook him again. "He'll have to wake up."

"But what if he doesn't wake up?" Diana asked, panic edging into her voice. "What will we do then?"

"Then we'll stay with him," Francesca told her. "He's our father."

"Can't we take him outside? It's getting hot in here."

"And what do you think they'll do to us if we take him out there?" Francesca asked. "We were going kill them. Do you think they'll just go away and leave us alone? Do you think they'll help us with him?"

Phoebe said, "But we can't stay here. We can't—"

"Yes, we can," Francesca said, cutting her off.

Brenna started crying harder.

Rachel heard none of what they said. She lay near the wall where she had fallen after Hope had put a knee into her face, breaking her nose and snapping her head back so that it hit the side of a chair very hard, hard enough to put a hairline crack in her skull.

She was still breathing, but only barely, and had no idea of what was going on around her.

Occasionally her face twitched, like the face of a woman having a disconcerting dream.

Perhaps she was dreaming of a different fire, one that she had watched from outside the house, one in which two people had died.

Perhaps she was dreaming of their screams.

The Prescotts and the Evanses were huddled together about twenty yards from the porch when Eli came coughing and choking out the front door, dragging the inert Reverend Woodley along by both arms.

Eli stopped short of the steps. He'd gone about as far as he could go. Francesca had reopened his wound with her elbow, and though Woodley was a small man, his deadweight still seemed plenty to Eli.

He looked back over his shoulder at the people in the yard. "I could use a little help here," he said.

Kenneth Prescott walked over quickly, with William Evans right behind. They stepped up on the porch, and each man took one of Woodley's arms.

Eli let go. "Better get him on out in the yard," he told them, wiping smoke and sweat from his forehead with his shirtsleeve.

"Is he still alive?" Prescott asked, looking at the large, dark stain on the back of Woodley's coat.

Eli walked down the steps. "How the hell do I know? All I did was bring him out of there. If you want to leave him on the porch, go ahead. He ain't my preacher."

Chastened, Prescott helped Evans lift the minister and carry him out into the yard. They turned him over and laid him on his back on the wet ground that would no doubt freeze again if the night got much colder. The stain on the front of Woodley's shirt was larger than the one on his coat.

Sue Beth Prescott knelt down and put her head next to Woodley's open mouth. "He's still breathing," she announced. "Where's Dr. Baxter?"

"Where do you think?" Eli said testily, looking back at the burning house.

He didn't really have anything against the two couples, even if they had more or less run out on everybody. He didn't much blame them for that, but he wished they'd stop asking him such stupid questions.

"What about the Ranger?" one of them asked.

"Him, too," Eli said. He decided that he might as well explain further. "Luther took Dr. Baxter upstairs. Cody went after them."

Everyone was looking at the house now. The fire had spread to cover most of the first floor. It flickered through the windows and lit up the darkness. Now and then a windowpane shattered like a gunshot from the heat. Thick smoke curled up into the night sky. The heat pressed against them like a giant hand, and they moved farther back, taking Woodley along with them.

"Do you think Mr. Cody can save the doctor?" Nancy Evans asked tremulously.

Eli was still watching the house. "Damned if I know."

• • •

Luther was reaching to tear off the front of Hope's shirt when Cody barreled into the room. He charged across the floor and leapt through the air, crashing into Luther and carrying him off the bed to the floor on the opposite side.

Luther bellowed with pain, but the anguish he felt seemed to lend him even greater strength. He threw Cody off and away from him almost as if the Ranger were as light as a feather pillow.

Cody bounced off the dresser, dazed but not seriously hurt. As Luther came at him, he got his first real look at the severe burns covering the giant's chest and shoulders. Even a quick glance was enough to tell him that if Luther didn't receive medical treatment quickly, he wouldn't survive for long.

But despite his wounds—or maybe because of them; Cody knew that life-threatening situations sometimes imparted almost superhuman strength, a surge from some wellspring of desperation—Luther remained incredibly strong, still strong enough even if he was dying to squash Cody like a bug if Cody let him.

Cody didn't intend to let him.

He rushed Luther and jabbed his face, snapping the big man's head back. But though Luther was horribly injured, he hadn't lost his quickness—or his strength as yet. Instead of trying to hit Cody back or dodge him, he simply grabbed the Ranger's arm and heaved him across the room.

Cody had never thought much about what flying would be like, but now he knew. He sailed several feet before he hit the wall. He rebounded and fell facedown on the floor. His head had taken about all it could take lately, and his mind seemed about to sink into some dark, deep pit.

Luther kicked him in the side, cracking a rib, but the pain had an unexpectedly beneficial effect. It woke Cody up. As Luther was about to kick him again, Cody grabbed the foot and twisted, hoping to bring Luther down. Luther was too strong, however, and he wrenched his foot free, managing at the same time to give Cody a gritty taste of the sole of his boot.

Cody's head rang like a supper bell, and he fell back against the wall.

Leering, Luther leaned down to finish him off. He would've succeeded if Hope hadn't thrown herself on his back, raking his crisped skin with her nails and pulling at his wild, bushy hair.

Luther let out a roar. By now so blinded by pain and confusion that he had forgotten why he had brought her there in the first place—or if he remembered, he no longer cared—he shook Hope from his back like a bull shaking off a bothersome fly. Then he picked her up and tried to toss her out the doorway into the hall.

She didn't make it. Her head hit the doorframe, and she fell to the floor.

Luther turned back to Cody. The Ranger had recovered slightly, thanks to the reprieve granted him by Hope's intervention, but instead of getting up, he lay where he was, pretending to be unconscious, watching from beneath his nearly closed eyelids as Luther advanced toward him. When Luther started to bend down to finish Cody off, probably by choking him or breaking his neck, Cody kicked him in the face with both feet, putting all the strength of his legs into it.

He felt cartilage crumple and teeth break as Luther howled and stumbled backward across the room. Cody almost felt sorry for him. Almost, but not quite. Not even one damned bit.

He struggled to his feet and took hold of the wooden chair that sat by the dresser.

Luther, bellowing like an enraged buffalo, rushed to meet him, but Cody smashed him with the chair and sent him staggering backward again. Luther stopped just short of the room's only window.

Holding the chair with the legs straight out in front of him, Cody ran at Luther. The chair struck Luther's chest, and Cody shoved hard, using his momentum to force Luther back.

Luther slammed into the window, shattering the glass and falling out with a long howl of rage and pain. The last

thing Cody saw of him was his bootheels. He didn't take
the time to look out and watch him hit the ground; he had
more important things to do.

Rushing to where a groggy Hope was trying to sit up,
Cody helped her and then asked if she could stand. She
didn't say anything for a second, and Cody feared he
might have to try to carry her. Ordinarily she wouldn't
have been much of a burden to him, but right now he
didn't think he could carry a kitten down the two flights
of stairs.

He was beginning to get anxious when Hope said, "I
think I'm all right now," and got shakily to her feet.

"Then let's get the hell out of here," Cody said, but even
as they started down the hall he could see the smoke boil-
ing up the stairs. The fire had reached the second floor.

Hope saw it, too. "What are we going to do?"

"This way," Cody said, leading her back into Luther's
room.

There was a washstand near the dresser, and, remarkably, the pitcher hadn't been knocked off it. Cody whipped
off his bandanna and handed it to Hope.

"Soak that and tie it around your face," he said.

He began ripping a strip of sheet from Luther's bed for
his own use. It smelled terrible, and the water didn't make
it smell any sweeter. When they were both masked, Cody
splashed what was left of the water on their clothing, and
they started out of the room again.

"Will that help?" Hope asked in a muffled voice.

Cody didn't really know. "Better than nothing," he said,
for whatever comfort that gave.

They got down the stairs to the second floor without too
much trouble. Fortunately, the stairway to the third floor
was on the opposite end of the hall from the one leading
from the ground floor to the second, so while the smoke
was thick, the fire hadn't yet reached the stairs.

But when they reached the second floor, they could feel
the floorboards cracking beneath their feet as they raced
along the hallway to the stairs leading down to the first
floor. Sparks shot through the air; flames licked along the
walls and roared along the ceiling. The wet cloths around
Cody's and Hope's faces were drying rapidly.

Just as they reached the head of the stairs, a charred board snapped beneath Cody's right foot. He sank down to his hip. Hope took his hands and struggled to pull him free, but he was stuck fast.

"You go on!" he shouted. "I'll get out and follow you." It was hard to hear himself over the roaring of the flames.

Hope looked over her shoulder at the stairway, which was nearly completely blocked by the fire.

"I'd just as soon stay here with you as try to get through that by myself," she said with a small laugh.

Anybody who could joke under such conditions was a hell of a woman, Cody thought. He wished he could bring himself to say something cheerful back to her, but he was too busy trying to wrench his leg out of the floor's grip. His hands pressed against hot boards that seemed to be just about at the flash point, and he pushed awkwardly with his free leg.

"It's no use," he said, but just as he said it, the trapped leg came free.

"Thank God," Hope breathed.

There was a long rip in Cody's pants, and he'd ripped some of the skin off his leg as well, but he didn't much care. All he could think about was getting Hope down those stairs. He took her hand and went forward.

The heat was so intense that it singed their hair and eyebrows. They couldn't touch the railing or the wall, and they could almost feel the stairs being incinerated beneath their feet.

"Go!" Cody yelled, giving Hope a weak shove. "Stay close to the wall and don't stop for anything!"

Hope plunged down the stairs with Cody right behind her. The fire was so hot now that their skin was nearly blistered, but Cody thought they were going to make it.

They were almost to the bottom of the stairs when his shirt burst into flame.

Because Luther's room was on the back side of the house—so that any unwary visitor wouldn't look up and notice anyone in his window—none of those watching from the front yard had seen him fall. They were all assuming the worst about Cody and Hope.

"I don't think they're coming out," Nancy Evans said, and Eli wondered if she was feeling guilty about running out and not trying to help anybody else. "Do you suppose that horrible Luther has done something to them? Shouldn't someone go in and help them?"

Eli wanted to ask her just who she had in mind for the "someone," but he didn't. He said, "Ma'am, couldn't nobody go in there."

"But they're going to die!" she said. "William, can't you do anything?"

Her husband shook his head. "I wish I could, but Mr. Peyton's right. There's no way that—"

His words were cut off by the sound of gunshots that seemed to be coming from the dining room.

"What's that?" Nancy asked, gripping her husband's arm. "Is someone shooting?"

"Could be," Eli said.

He didn't really know. It was possible that the sisters had killed themselves rather than face death in the fire or face what the law would do to them when Cody got them to Del Rio. On the other hand, it was possible that the fire was causing the cartridges to explode without any help from anyone. Eli wasn't sure it made much difference at this point.

"What about the preacher?" he asked Sue Beth Prescott, who'd been tending Woodley's wound as best she could.

"The bleeding's stopped," she said. "I think the bullet just went right through his shoulder. His breathing's regular, but I don't know what else to do for him."

"We'll just have to do the best we can," Eli said as he watched the burning house. "Hopefully, Cody'll bring Dr. Baxter out safely, and then she can tend to the preacher." But he didn't really believe that would happen. Not with so much flame and smoke and not after so much time had passed.

Eli stared at the front door, thinking that this was all that damn Gus's fault. If he'd just kept away from Eli's cabin, then none of this would've happened. How many people had died? Eli didn't care to count. That damn

Gus was always no good, but this just about took the cake.

Still, if what Cody had said was true, Gus had gotten pretty much what he deserved. Maybe even more than he deserved. At least those Carswells hadn't eaten him. It was just as well for them that they hadn't. He probably would've given them a stomachache.

Eli hated to go in the barn, since he guessed Gus was in there, but they were going to have to do something about spending the night, and it looked like none of them had any idea of what. Looked like Eli was elected to make the decisions.

He thought they'd be all right outside for a while, and that was just as well, since everybody seemed to like to watch a fire. There was something about watching a house as big as that one burn that just seemed to fascinate folks. It was too bad about Cody and Dr. Baxter. They were both nice folks, and they didn't deserve to die in such an awful way.

Eli brushed at his eyes. Damn that Gus, anyway.

He had completely given up hope of seeing either Cody or Dr. Baxter again when the burning man came stumbling out the door.

CHAPTER
||||||||||||||||||||||||||| **18** |||||||||||||||||||||||||||

When his shirt caught on fire, Cody didn't waste any time thinking about it. He knew that the front door was only a few steps away, and though he couldn't see it, he knew its general direction.

"Follow me!" he yelled, praying that Hope could hear him, and if she could, that she could see him well enough to follow.

Summoning up his last reserves of strength, he ran to where he hoped the front door was. Almost before he knew it, he was through the opening, across the porch, and rolling on the cold, wet ground, spinning over and over to extinguish the fire that had almost destroyed his shirt.

Hope had followed rapidly and was right beside him, helping him to roll. Her own clothing had survived, thanks to the fact that Cody had splashed most of the water from the pitcher on her instead of on himself.

When the fire was out, Cody struggled to his feet with Hope's assistance. He told her, "We've got to move back from the house."

Eli was there to take his arm and lead them over to the others. "I sure never thought I'd see either one of you again," the rancher said. "I thought you'd both be burnt like bacon in there." He looked at them critically in the eerie glow emanating from the fire and the moon. "Course I could've been right. You look pretty well scorched, sure enough."

Cody, his eyes red and smarting from the smoke, looked at Hope. Her face was smeared with soot, and there were grimy tracks down her cheeks from tears caused by the smoke. Her clothes were torn, and the ends of her blond hair were singed into tight, tiny curls.

"Do I look as bad as you?" Cody asked with a smile.

Hope wrinkled her nose at him. "Worse. At least I didn't lose my shirt. Well, not all of it, anyway."

"I still have part of mine," Cody retorted. "It's just a little burned." But he could see that it was worse than a little burned. There were more gaping, charred holes than there was fabric.

He started to say something else, but Hope suddenly noticed the Reverend Woodley. "Is he alive?" she asked.

"Yep," Eli said. "Miz Prescott did all she could for him, but he needs a real doctor."

Hope knelt and began tending to him.

Cody and Eli turned back and looked at the house. It was being quickly consumed by the conflagration, and the timbers were popping and groaning. Flames had reached the roof, and the orange glow against the black sky seemed to light up half the horizon. As they watched, one of the brick chimneys collapsed inside the structure and rumbled down the burning walls.

"What about the Carswells?" Cody asked.

"We didn't see 'em come out, so I reckon they're still in there," Eli said.

"And Rachel?"

Eli rubbed his jaw. The back of his hand scraped on his whiskers. "She's still in there, too."

Hope somehow heard that remark over the roaring fire, and she stood up from her attentions to Woodley. "We've got to get her out."

"We can't," Cody said. "We can't go back in there." He indicated his shirt with his hand.

Hope wasn't watching. She started running for the house.

She had reached the porch by the time Cody caught up with her. He grabbed her shoulder to stop her from rushing inside and pulled her back to safety. Just inside the door, flames jumped higher than his head.

"You can't save her!" Cody cried over the roar of the blaze. "It's too late."

"I've got to try," Hope told him. "It's my fault that she's in there."

"What are you talking about? How could it be your fault?"

"I kicked her in the face. She was probably unconscious and couldn't get out by herself. I've got to save her."

Cody shook his head. "It's not a bit your fault. She had a choice, and she picked the side she wanted to be on. Otherwise you wouldn't have had to kick her." He was gradually leading Hope away from the house. "You've got to help the preacher. He's the one who needs you."

Hope allowed herself to be removed to where Woodley was lying, but she kept looking back at the house.

"I should have done something," she said. "I should have helped her."

"That's the doctor talking again," Cody said gently. "And the preacher needs a doctor more than Rachel does."

"Maybe you're right," Hope said. "But still . . ." Her voice trailed off, and she turned to see what she could do for Woodley.

The inside of the house was an inferno.

Francesca didn't know what had become of her sisters, though she had a pretty good idea that they were dead. She knew that they'd given up on her attempts to revive their father and had deserted her. They had tried to find a way out of the dining room, but she didn't think any of them had been successful. She'd heard their screams as the fire trapped them and consumed them.

She had finally decided to move her father to the kitchen, where the flames for some reason hadn't reached as yet.

Unfortunately, as soon as she had dragged him into the other room, the fire spread there, crawling inexorably across the floor to where she cowered behind the big cast-iron stove. Only a few minutes after she got there, the stove was sizzling hot from the blaze that now burned on three sides of it and above it.

"What are we going to do?" Francesca asked her father, who still wasn't answering any questions. She wished her sisters were there. They hadn't been much help, but at least they would talk to her.

She looked around the room at the flames that danced everywhere, even on the ceiling now. Dark shadows jumped around in the red and orange flames, and sparks fell from above to light new fires everywhere. Francesca's skin was blistered and her eyes and mouth were scorched and dry from the ferocious heat.

Maybe she could make it to the back door and get away, she thought. It was possible that no one would see her leave. She didn't know where she would go, but anywhere would be better than where she was at that moment.

She thought about her father. Maybe he wouldn't mind if she left him there. Surely he'd understand.

She stood up just as the ceiling fell in. A burning support beam struck her head and drove her down. She fell across her father's body and had time for one last despairing look into his bulging eyes. That was the last she ever knew.

"There she goes," Eli said as the huge structure collapsed.

It seemed to fall inward upon itself, everything happening in a rush, the roof sinking suddenly, pulling the walls along with it, everything coming down with a crash and a roar that sent flames and sparks flying high into the night sky. When it was over, there was nothing left standing except for parts of two chimneys and one wall. Much of the fire was snuffed by the wreckage, but flames still leapt here and there, and Cody knew that the rubble would smolder for days.

"You don't reckon anybody's left alive in all that mess, do you?" Eli said.

Cody shook his head. It simply wasn't possible. Anyone not burned to death or suffocated by the smoke would have been killed by falling debris.

"What about that Luther?" Eli asked. "What'd you do with him?"

Cody hadn't thought about Luther since sending him out the window. "He fell out the third-floor window.

Maybe I'd better go make sure he won't be bothering us."

Cody started around the house with Eli at his heels. The Ranger was beginning to feel the cold now, but somehow he didn't mind. It was better than the heat he'd felt just a short while before. It was going to be a while before he'd want to pull his chair up close to a fireplace again, no matter how cold he got.

Luther's body was lying a few feet away from what was left of the back wall of the house. He was lying on his back, and his head was twisted at an unnatural angle.

"Broke his neck, looks like," Eli said, standing over him.

Cody thought so, too. Luther wouldn't be any more trouble to them.

Eli inspected the body. "Face looks like hell, too, but I don't guess that killed him. You reckon we ought to just leave him here?"

"I don't see why not. Ground's probably too hard for us to dig a grave." He shrugged. "Maybe tomorrow we'll move him."

Eli was agreeable to that. Actually, he didn't much care if they buried Luther or not. Let the buzzards have him. "What about the ones you said're in the barn?" he asked.

Cody hadn't given that much thought, but it was something they'd have to deal with, especially if the weather got any warmer. He said as much to Eli.

"Right now, though," he added, "the problem is what we're going to do for the rest of the night."

"I guess we could spend the night in the barn," Eli said. "I don't much cotton to that idea myself, what with those bodies bein' in there, but I don't see what else we can do."

Cody didn't, either. "Let's see about that preacher first," he said.

They walked back around the smoldering ruin.

"How's Mr. Woodley?" Cody asked Hope.

"He's awake now. The wound's not bad, but it would help if we had something to bandage it with besides Sue Beth's petticoat. And it would be nice, too, if we had some antiseptic to clean it with."

"If Carswell had any livestock to take care of," Cody said, "which I doubt, there might be something in the barn."

"Oh," Nancy Evans said, "I don't think I want to go in there."

"We have to spend the night somewhere," Cody reminded her. "We need to get out of the cold. There'll be some horse blankets in there that we can wrap up in."

He didn't even mention the possibility of building a fire. He figured that the others weren't any more ready for that than he was.

Evans and Prescott helped Woodley to his feet and supported him as everyone started toward the barn. Cody thought Sue Beth and Nancy would be all right as long as they stayed out of the tack room. Somebody would have to go in there, however, to fetch the blankets and look for antiseptic. He could do it if no one else volunteered; he'd already seen what else was in there.

They were just entering the barn when Cody heard something.

Eli heard it, too. "Horses comin'," he said. "Lot of 'em."

Cody hurried the others inside the barn and closed the door. He and Eli would stay outside to see who was coming—not that there was much they'd be able to do if the riders happened to be more friends of Gus or, worse than that, friends of the Carswells.

Cody's mind was relieved almost as soon as the riders came in sight. Riding in front was Alan Northrup.

When the horsemen reached them and reined in, Cody was grinning broadly. He had never been quite so happy to see anything as he was to see the stocky young Ranger's honest, smiling face.

"Howdy, Alan. I'm mighty glad to see you."

Alan studied Cody's disheveled appearance. "Hey, Cody. You, too, Mr. Peyton. I'm mighty glad to see the both of you. You look like you've had quite a time of it."

"That's the truth," Cody acknowledged. "What on earth are you doing way out here?"

"Looking for you. Cap'n Vickery expected you back a few days ago, and Dr. Baxter's been giving him puredee hell about his missing niece. Said he'd trusted her to the Rangers, and now she was probably dead on the prairie somewhere. Both of 'em have been in an all-fired tizzy for the last couple of days 'cause it was too icy for anybody to go looking for you. When it cleared up today, they had the company out first thing."

"How'd you ever find this place?" Cody asked.

Alan laughed. "Well, it sure wasn't the first place we looked. We went to your cabin, Mr. Peyton, but there wasn't anybody there. After that we just sort of wandered here and there, looking around till it was time to make camp. We'd just finished our supper when somebody saw a red glow in the sky that looked like a big fire. We got curious, and here we are."

By now the others had come out of the barn. "Looks like you found yourself some other folks that had a little trouble with the weather," Alan said. "Not to mention a little trouble with matches."

Cody managed a weary grin. "That's not all."

Alan looked around, puzzled. "What else?" he asked.

"We found out there's a lot worse things than a little cold weather," Cody answered. As he spoke, Hope stepped to his side, and he slipped an arm around her. "We found out a few other things, too."

Alan eyed them pointedly. "Looks like you did," he said with a chuckle. "And it looks like the two of you could use a couple of new shirts. Maybe we can round up some extras."

"We were just going in the barn to try to get warm," Cody said. "Figure there'll be horse blankets in there. We have a wounded man in there, too. Did you bring a medical kit?"

"I expect we did," Alan said. He signaled for the men to dismount and slid out of the saddle himself. "Why don't you and the rest of the folks go inside and warm up while we see what we've got for you?" he said to Cody.

Cody suggested to Hope that she go in with the others; he wanted to warn Alan about what he'd found out and about what was in the tack room. She gave Cody a quick kiss and started toward the barn.

Cody turned back to Alan. "I've got quite a story to tell you, my friend. But I wouldn't mind first taking you up on that offer of another shirt so I can warm up a little."

Alan's shoulders began to shake with laughter. "Ah, Cody, things'll *really* warm up for you when you get back to Del Rio and a certain redheaded hostess finds out about that lady sawbones. . . ."

CODY'S LAW: BOOK 10

A GALLOWS WAITING

by Matthew S. Hart

Texas Ranger Sam Cody has finally gotten the break he's been waiting for in tracking the rustlers who've been plaguing the border region; with a young rancher riding alongside him, he closes in. The fight is brief and bloody, leaving all six rustlers dead and Cody and the rancher wounded.

Returning to Del Rio, Cody plans to report in, then to rest and let his wounds heal. But headquarters is empty. A note from Captain Vickery explains that the rest of Company C is out on patrol, and he's gone to catch the stage-coach to San Angelo—and the person responsible for a string of murders. The next morning Cody gets a telegram from the sheriff of a town on the stage line: Vickery has been attacked by the killer he sought to apprehend. Cody rides to El Dorado and finds Vickery recuperating from minor knife wounds but anxious to get back into action.

Determined to find the killer, the two Rangers team up on an assignment that quickly turns into a nightmare. "We're goin' after that madman and bring him in for a proper hangin'—even if we got to follow him to hell and back!" Vickery says. But as the number of horribly mutilated bodies mounts and the killer continues to elude the Rangers, it looks as if the captain may have come closer to the truth than he realizes.

Read A GALLOWS WAITING, on sale
wherever Bantam Books are sold.